A JUICY STEAK TRAGEDY

AN IVY CREEK COZY MYSTERY

RUTH BAKER

CLEANTALES PUBLISHING

Copyright © CleanTales Publishing

First published in February 2023

All characters and events in this publication, other than those clearly in the public domain, are fictitious and any resemblance to real persons, living or dead, is purely coincidental.

Copyright © CleanTales Publishing

The moral right of the author has been asserted.

All rights reserved. This book or any portion thereof may not be reproduced or used in any manner whatsoever without the express written permission of the publisher except for the use of brief quotations in a book review.

For questions and comments about this book, please contact
info@cleantales.com

ISBN: 9798376643938
Imprint: Independently Published

OTHER BOOKS IN THE IVY CREEK SERIES

Which Pie Goes with Murder?

Twinkle, Twinkle, Deadly Sprinkles

Eat Once, Die Twice

Silent Night, Unholy Bites

Waffles and Scuffles

Cookie Dough and Bruised Egos

A Sticky Toffee Catastrophe

Dough Shall Not Murder

Deadly Bites on Winter Nights

A Juicy Steak Tragedy

AN IVY CREEK COZY MYSTERY

BOOK TEN

1

Key in hand, Lucy paused for a moment outside Sweet Delights Bakery to admire the front window display she and her crew had finished yesterday. Valentine's Day was right around the corner, and the shop was all decked out for the occasion.

A mockup of a three-tiered wedding cake took center stage, surrounded by white gauzy tulle and pearl strands. Heart-shaped balloons floated on glitzy ribbons, rising from behind a small table adorned with a ruffled tablecloth in pink. A silver platter set on top was stacked with Valentine's Day cookies – heart shaped and sporting sentimental messages. Tiny paper hearts and confetti dotted the red silk fabric they'd used as the floor covering.

Lucy smiled as she unlocked the front door and flipped on the lights. Valentine's Day was one of her favorite holidays in the bakery, both because she found the red and pink color scheme cheery in the midst of winter–and the fact that chocolate was the signature sweet. How could you go wrong with chocolate?

As Lucy stepped inside, she noticed someone had pushed a flyer under the door while they were closed. She picked it up and studied it curiously. The bell jangled at her shoulder as Hannah, her number one employee, let herself in.

"Brrrr!" Hannah rubbed her mittened hands together. "A good day to work in front of the ovens!" She peered at the flyer Lucy held. "What's that?"

Lucy read the bold type at the top. "It's advertising that new restaurant that opened a few weeks ago - Sizzle." She glanced at Hannah, "Been there yet?"

Hannah shook her head. "I've been sticking close to home, but my Mom and Dad went the first week it opened, and they raved about the flavor of their steak and chicken. I guess Sizzle's got a kickin' marinade!"

Lucy cocked an eyebrow. "Better than Wrigley's?"

Wrigley's Steakhouse was an Ivy Creek icon that had been around for decades. Wrigley's claim to fame was their family marinade recipe that had been passed down through three generations. It was a closely guarded secret, one that Lionel Wrigley, the owner, refused to share – even when interviewed by a popular foodie magazine last year.

Hannah nodded as she scanned the advertised specials on the flyer. "According to my mom, yes." She looked at Lucy. "Looks yummy! You should get Taylor to take you for Valentine's Day."

The two turned as the door opened again.

"Hello, hello," Betsy came breezing in, her cheeks pink from the cold, and her eyes sparkling. "What a lovely morning!"

Lucy's youngest employee had a glow about her, as she'd had almost continuously for the past six months that she'd been dating Joseph Hiller, Ivy Creek's local theater director. The two were almost inseparable, and Lucy suspected there would be wedding bells within the next year.

"Good morning," Lucy held up the flyer for Betsy to see. "Have you guys been to Sizzle yet? They have some great appetizers and entrees listed."

Betsy hung up her coat and retrieved her apron from behind the counter. She shook her head.

"We've been working around the clock on this production," she said. "I'm so glad I volunteered to help backstage. Just the costuming alone is so intense... and don't even get me started on the scenery! Thank goodness we have a bunch of college kids helping out."

The Ivy Creek Theater was putting on a production of Romeo and Juliet, just in time for Valentine's Day. The whole town was buzzing about it.

"Isn't opening night tonight?" asked Hannah, pouring herself a cup of coffee.

Betsy grinned and nodded. "It is! You guys should come."

Lucy shook her head as she set up the cappuccino machine. "I promised Aunt Tricia we'd go together, and she has her book club tonight. But we're planning to come soon."

Betsy nodded, though she looked disappointed. "Hannah? How about you? If you don't want to sit by yourself in the audience, you can come watch from backstage with me. It'll be fun!"

Hannah busied herself with a notepad, taking stock of what pastries needed to be baked today. "Hmm. Probably not, but thanks."

Betsy cast a puzzled look at Lucy, who shrugged. Although Lucy had her own theory why Hannah didn't want to go, it wasn't her place to bring it up.

"OK," Betsy said. "Let me know if you change your mind." She looked at the clock. "Isn't Tricia working today?" Lucy's Aunt Tricia was never late, and it was almost time to open the doors.

Lucy nodded. "She stopped at the bank first. She should be here any minute." As she said the words, Aunt Tricia's blue sedan pulled into the parking lot. "Oh, there she is!"

"Oh, good." Betsy ducked down behind the counter for a minute, then popped back up. "I'm just going to go get another roll of register tape. Be right back."

She headed for the staircase to the upper level, where Lucy's office and the stockroom were located, along with a large veranda for dining in the warm weather.

When Betsy was out of earshot, Lucy approached Hannah. "You can come to the play with me and Aunt Tricia, you know. I'm not even sure if Taylor's going to come. It could be a girls' night out."

Hannah offered a small smile. "Maybe. Thanks."

Lucy studied her friend, not sure if she was overstepping. "Hannah, I hope you're not going to avoid the theater forever because of..." Lucy stopped speaking as Hannah's eyes widened.

"Miles," Hannah whispered. She looked alarmed.

Lucy frowned. "Yes. That's what I was going to say. Just because Miles didn't accept your invitation on New Year's Eve—"

"No!" Hannah hissed. "He's here! Miles is here!" She jutted her chin at the front window overlooking the parking lot.

Lucy turned and saw Aunt Tricia walking across the parking lot, chatting with Miles Clifton, Joseph's new assistant. Hannah had met Miles a few months ago, and Lucy had seen instantly that her friend had a crush on the strapping red-haired man. Especially once they'd found out Miles was actively involved with animal rescue, fostering stray dogs until they found forever homes. Hannah was known to have a giant soft spot when it came to animals.

At Lucy's urging, Hannah had invited Miles out for a drink on New Year's Eve. Lucy had been quite surprised to hear from Hannah that Miles had politely declined. Shy already, Hannah was mortified at the turn of events and had been avoiding the theater ever since.

"Hannah..." Lucy turned back, but Hannah had gone, disappearing into the kitchen.

The bell jangled, and Aunt Tricia preceded Miles into the bakery.

"Look who I found, out in the freezing weather, without even a hat or gloves!" Aunt Tricia bustled in behind the counter, dropping her purse and snagging two coffee cups.

"Black, or cream and sugar?" she asked Miles, picking up the coffeepot.

He smiled, showing straight, and even, white teeth. "Black, please," he said.

Miles looked to Lucy, next, with a friendly expression. "Hi, Lucy. How goes it?" His eyes met hers, then flickered away, roaming around the bakery.

"I'm good!" Lucy smiled. "Are you all ready for opening night?"

His green eyes twinkled as he responded to her with good humor. "As ready as we're going to be."

Once again, Miles glanced around, peering over Lucy's shoulder in the direction of the kitchen.

"Is Hannah around?"

2

*L*ucy stalled, unsure of how to answer. "Uh… yes, she's… hang on, let me see where she is."

Lucy turned and ducked through the entryway leading to the kitchen. Hannah was nowhere to be seen. Puzzled, Lucy turned the corner and saw the walk-in cooler door was open. Crossing the room, she peered inside the refrigeration unit, finding Hannah standing there, armed with a notepad and pen.

"What are you doing?" Lucy asked, perplexed. Hannah usually baked morning pastries first thing before she tackled anything else.

"Inventory," Hannah replied, without looking up. "I didn't want to wait until the end of the month. We may have a big Valentine's rush, you know."

Lucy wasn't fooled by her friend's explanation. "Hmm. Well, Miles just asked to see you."

Hannah looked up, panic in her blue eyes. "What? Why? What does he want?"

Lucy shook her head. "I don't know. Maybe he just wants to say hi."

Hannah frowned, then looked back down at her pad. "Please tell him I'm in the middle of inventory." She peeked up at Lucy, and Lucy's heart softened at the vulnerable expression on her face.

"OK," Lucy agreed. After all, it wouldn't be a bad thing for Miles to have to chase Hannah a little, she thought.

Lucy walked back out to the front, where Miles was chatting with Betsy about opening night.

"Hey, Miles, Hannah's right in the middle of inventory, so she asked if you could please leave a message."

Betsy swiveled around to regard Lucy with a puzzled look on her face. She opened her mouth to speak, and Lucy caught her eye with a meaningful look.

Miles looked nonplussed. "Uh, OK..." He drummed his fingers on the counter. "Could you just tell her I stopped by to say hello?"

Lucy nodded. "Sure." She smiled to put him at ease. "Have a great opening night!"

Miles thanked her and wrapped up his conversation with Betsy, taking his leave a moment later. As soon as the door shut behind him, Betsy turned to face Lucy.

"What was that all about? Why wouldn't Hannah come out to say hello?"

Lucy saw Aunt Tricia had turned to regard her with an inquisitive expression.

Lucy held up her hands. "You guys have questions. You should go ask Hannah. I need to pop out for a few minutes to pick up a few things at Bing's Grocery. Be back soon."

She made herself a latte for the road and grabbed her purse, heading out just as Hannah reappeared and was immediately barraged by questions from the ladies.

Chuckling and shaking her head, Lucy settled herself into her SUV and headed into town.

———

Lucy pushed her cart through the aisles at Bing's, stocking up on this and that. Although she ordered her flour and sugar through a wholesale supplier, she liked to shop locally as much as she could.

She turned her cart down the next aisle and almost collided with another shopper.

"Oh, sorry!"

"My apologies.'

Lucy smiled at the pleasant-looking man, who she judged to be in his early forties. She'd never seen him before. She glanced into his cart, mildly curious at the strange assortment he'd gathered. A dozen jars of crushed garlic, several quart bottles of cider vinegar, an array of a multitude of spices, and two gallons of extra-virgin olive oil.

He must have caught her looking, because he grinned, offering, "Shopping for my restaurant."

Lucy looked up sharply, eyebrows raised. "Sizzle restaurant?" Ivy Creek was small enough that Lucy knew all the other restaurant owners on sight.

He nodded, looking pleased, and offered his hand. "Yes. I'm Oliver Crenshaw. Pleased to meet you."

Lucy shook his hand, glad to make his acquaintance. "Lucy Hale, owner of Sweet Delights Bakery."

Oliver grinned. "A bakery! I'll have to come by and visit."

She fished out a business card and handed it to him. "Please do! And, by the way, I just received your flyer this morning, and I'm intrigued. I'll definitely be stopping by Sizzle soon."

Oliver's eyes crinkled as he tucked away her business card. "Excellent! I'll be watching for you." Another shopper came up behind him, and so he continued down the aisle, calling over his shoulder, "Have a good day!"

Lucy waved goodbye and studied her own cart. *That should do it for now.* She wheeled over to the checkout, thankful there was no line.

The cashier cracked her bubblegum loudly as she scanned Lucy's items. "That Crenshaw fellow has got himself on the wrong side of Lionel Wrigley already." Obviously, she'd seen Lucy chatting with Oliver.

"You don't say…" Lucy replied distractedly, scrabbling through her purse for her customer rewards card.

"Yup." The cashier began to bag Lucy's purchases. "Wrigley made a big scene in here last week. Bumped into Crenshaw in aisle three, started yelling that Crenshaw had stolen his marinade recipe. We had to get the store manager out here to talk him down."

Lucy stared at her in disbelief. "Stolen? How on earth could he have stolen Wrigley's recipe?"

The young woman shook her head, accepting the money Lucy held out. "Now, that I don't know. I hear Wrigley's keeps their recipe locked up tight. My cousin Bobby worked at Wrigley's as a prep cook, and he said only Chef Fugasi is allowed to make the special marinade."

Lucy sniffed dismissively. "Wrigley's is probably just jealous that there's another steakhouse in town."

She gathered her bags and headed out, wondering if Ivy Creek was big enough for two steakhouses. *Competition wasn't a bad thing,* she thought. *Keeps everyone on their best game.*

———

THE NEXT MORNING, Lucy and Hannah were baking in companionable silence, the scent of apple-cinnamon bread filling the air. Lucy knew Hannah well enough to know her friend didn't want to discuss the visit from Miles yesterday. Although Lucy would love for Hannah to find someone special who made her happy, it would happen when the time was right. Pushing wasn't going to make it happen more quickly.

The bell jangled out front and moments later they heard Betsy's voice, calling out from the front before she'd even appeared in the archway.

"You guys wouldn't believe what happened last night!"

Betsy's eyes were wide as she rounded the corner, standing in the doorway of the kitchen.

Lucy looked at her with concern, noticing that Betsy seemed somewhat distressed. *Not good news, then.*

"Oh, no! Opening night. Did something go wrong?" Lucy hoped for Joseph's sake nothing terrible had happened. They'd worked so hard on this production.

Betsy waved a hand. "The play went fine. Full house. But what happened at the end... oh, my, it was so devastating! That poor man!"

Hannah stopped mixing cinnamon streusel and turned to look at Betsy, as well.

"Well? What was it? What happened?"

Betsy sighed dramatically. "You know, Bert Dobbins has the role of Romeo, right?"

Lucy nodded. Bert was a nice guy in his mid-twenties. He worked as a cook here and there, but his real passion was acting. She'd seen him perform before, and had to admit, he was pretty good. She was looking forward to seeing him play the lead in Romeo and Juliet.

At her nod, Betsy continued. "Bert did such an amazing job! Brought me to tears... and the crowd loved it! Even after everyone had taken their bows and left the stage, the audience called for Bert to come back out." She put her hand to her heart, her eyes misting over.

"Well, he came back out - with a rose in his hand. His girlfriend Daphne was there in the front row, and Bert had arranged for the lighting guy to shine a spotlight on her, and then..." her breath hitched. "And then..."

Lucy and Hannah waited as Betsy tried to control her emotions, her eyes shimmering.

She took a deep breath and blurted out, "He asked Daphne to marry him, right there, in front of all of those people!"

3

Lucy gasped, and heard Hannah say, "What??? Oh, my God!"

Betsy nodded and brushed at her eyes. She continued softly, "It was so romantic! But I guess Daphne didn't think so."

"Oh, no…" Lucy breathed, knowing what was coming.

Betsy shook her head sadly. "Daphne just froze, looking horrified at all the attention. Everyone was looking at her, and Bert… just standing there on stage, waiting for a response."

"What did she say?" asked Hannah, her voice hushed.

Betsy sighed. "She didn't say anything. After a minute she just stood up and ran out of the theater." She looked sad. "I think she was crying. I just feel so bad for both of them."

"Oh, wow," Lucy commented. "That's rough. I guess some things aren't meant to be so public." She tried to imagine herself in Daphne's place. Even if, hypothetically, she welcomed a marriage proposal, she'd rather it not be a public event.

"What about Bert? Is he going to be OK continuing as the lead in the play?" Hannah asked. "I imagine he's embarrassed, and you know this town…"

Ivy Creek was such a small town. Little things like this were never forgotten, Lucy thought. Poor Bert would have this follow him for years to come.

Betsy looked sober. "I know Joseph is planning to talk to him. Hopefully, he'll continue. He's such a good Romeo!"

She looked around, seeing the apple-cinnamon loaves all stacked neatly on the table. "That's what smells so good! Is the first batch ready to bag up yet?"

Lucy nodded, and Betsy got to work, bagging and tagging the bread, and prepping the front. Today was Aunt Tricia's day off and Betsy would be running the counter alone, although Lucy was planning to help with the lunch rush.

Hannah rolled out some sugar cookie dough and began cutting out heart shapes. "You know, it would be great if we could put custom messages on these cookies."

Typically, they would ice the heart cookies in red or pink royal icing and write simple two-word messages, such as "Love You" or "Be Mine".

Lucy measured some powdered sugar into a bowl, preparing to whip up another batch of icing. "Yeah… but they're a little too small to write more than what we're doing."

Hannah looked up, speculatively. "But do they have to be?"

Lucy blinked. "What do you mean?"

"Why can't we make larger cookies, maybe four-inch by six-inch rectangles, and write custom messages? We could decorate the edges with swirls and hearts, so it would still look like a Valentine, but people could request an entire sentence."

Lucy grinned, delighted by the idea. "Cookie-grams! And we could offer delivery as an option. I bet that would be a hit!"

Hannah looked pleased. "Hey, I could make up a few samples to put in the front window, if you want. And I bet Betsy would love to make a sign advertising them."

Lucy nodded enthusiastically, switching off the mixer. "That's a great idea, Hannah! I think Betsy might know of a few students who'd be willing to deliver them… and maybe get paid in pastries, instead of cash."

Hannah chuckled. "Oh, yes. I'm sure that would work. College students all seem to have bottomless stomachs."

Lucy smirked. "Ha! I believe the same has been said about you." Hannah was notorious for having a sweet tooth, and Lucy was envious of her friend's ability to eat sweets and not gain an ounce.

After the lunch rush, Lucy discussed the prospect with Betsy, who immediately fell in love with the idea.

"Oh, yes! Valentine Cookie-grams," Betsy declared, wiping down tables and discarding trash. "I might want to send one myself! Joseph loves your sugar cookies."

Lucy nodded, tapping numbers into a calculator. "I think they would sell really well. We just have to make sure we don't take more orders than we can get delivered. Do you think any of the college kids at the theater would want to deliver them? Maybe for bakery credit?"

Betsy nodded, picking up a magazine that a lunch customer had left behind. "I'm sure I can find at least two, if not three students to take that on."

She walked back toward the counter, leafing through the magazine. "Hey, Lucy, check this out."

Betsy spread the magazine open on the counter for Lucy to see the article.

Is He Mr. Right? Or Mr. Right-Now? Take the Soul Mate Compatibility Quiz

Lucy laughed out loud. "Twenty questions will tell you if he's Mr. Right?"

She shook her head at the silliness of it. Lucy had recently rekindled her romance with Ivy Creek's deputy sheriff, Taylor Baker. They'd once been childhood sweethearts but had drifted apart when she'd moved away to the city during college. In the past few months that she and Taylor had resumed dating, she'd felt closer than ever to him.

Betsy smiled, but she picked up a pen, none the less. "Well, it might be fun to see what it says." She started reading the questions out loud.

"Number one. When you plan to take a trip together, who makes the arrangements? Multiple choice: I do. They do. We discuss it and plan it together."

Lucy frowned. "What if you never take trips together?"

Betsy looked up from where she was recording her answers on a napkin. "Maybe you skip the question? Or just guess? If you did take a trip, who would plan it?"

She moved on to the second question while Lucy pondered that one. "When something exciting happens in your partner's life, do you hear about it from them first, or do you hear it from someone else they've told?"

Betsy marked down her own answer, while Lucy narrowed her eyes, trying to remember the last time either Taylor or she, herself, had exciting news. She was pretty sure she always told Taylor first… but what about him?

Betsy read the next question. "Do you feel that you and your partner are in sync with life's milestones, such as marriage and having kids?"

Betsy sighed, her eyes turning dreamy. "Joseph and I agree. Two kids would be perfect. But we'd want to wait a few years." She turned to look at Lucy with a soft smile.

"How about you and Taylor? I bet he wants a large family."

Lucy's mind went blank. *Did Taylor want a large family? Did he want kids at all?*

"Hmm." Lucy looked pensive. "I'm not sure we've ever talked about it." She chuckled dismissively. "I'm sure he wants whatever I want."

Betsy raised an eyebrow. "What if he doesn't? I mean, not to play devil's advocate, but what if he doesn't want marriage and kids?"

Her question was heard by Hannah, who came through the kitchen doorway at that moment, bearing a tray of brownies.

"Who doesn't want marriage and kids?"

Lucy blew out a breath, shaking her head. "No one. Nothing. We were talking hypothetically – whether or not Taylor and I want the same things from life."

"They've never even talked about marriage and kids," Betsy informed Hannah, who turned a surprised look on Lucy.

"Never? But you guys go way back." Hannah suddenly looked out the window. "Well, speak of the devil…"

Lucy glanced up and saw a familiar form making his way across the parking lot to the bakery.

Taylor.

4

Lucy flipped the magazine shut, pushing it to one side as the bell jangled.

"Hello, ladies." Taylor's blue eyes twinkled as he came through the bakery door. "Do I smell apple-cinnamon bread?"

His question was met with smiles all around. Taylor's sweet tooth was legendary, though you'd never guess it from his muscular physique.

"Second batch just came out of the oven," Betsy announced, as Lucy came around the counter to peck Taylor on the cheek. "Should I bag you one up to take home?"

Taylor grinned. "Two, please. I'll bring one by to my mother."

Lucy looked up into his face, her eyes concerned. "Is she feeling any better?" Taylor's mother had caught a cold weeks before, and Lucy knew he'd been worried when she'd come down with a wracking cough.

Taylor nodded, though his expression turned serious. "A little bit. I finally convinced her to make an appointment with the doctor."

Lucy sighed, relieved. "Oh, that's good." Mrs. Baker had caught pneumonia just last winter. Lucy was glad she'd agreed to get professional care this time, before her condition worsened.

She gave Taylor a quick squeeze around the waist before rounding the corner and pouring him a cup of coffee, black. She slid it across the counter.

"What's going on in town today?" she asked, studying his face.

Taylor sipped his coffee and met her eyes. "All everyone's talking about is Bert Dobbins." He looked over at Betsy. "Was it as bad as they're saying? The proposal at the theater?"

Betsy had finished bagging the fresh loaves and had now opened a drawer in search of twist ties. She nodded, her eyes full of compassion.

"It was so heartbreaking to watch," she said. "After Daphne ran out, Bert just stood there on the stage, like he didn't know what to do." She secured the bags with the ties and set two loaves in front of Taylor.

"Wow, that poor fellow. Bad luck, I guess." He shook his head. "That's a lot of pressure on a guy, the whole proposal thing on bended knee."

Lucy cocked her head. "What do you mean, on a guy? It's a lot of pressure on a girl, too, to decide whether to say yes or no, and maybe break someone's heart." She felt bad for Daphne, having been put on the spot like that. Bert should have known better.

"Doesn't compare," declared Taylor. "A rejection like that could really mess up a man."

Lucy frowned, opening her mouth to debate his point, when Betsy diverted Taylor's attention.

"Taylor, have you heard much about this new restaurant, Sizzle?" Betsy held up the flyer for him to see.

He shook his head, perusing the specials listed. "Looks interesting…"

"I met the owner the other day at Bing's Grocery," Lucy commented. "Oliver Crenshaw. A really nice guy."

Taylor looked her way. "Maybe we should give it a try this weekend. What do you think?"

Lucy smiled, pleased at the prospect. "Sure!"

Taylor glanced down at his watch. "I've got to get going. I'm giving a talk at the elementary school about Stranger Danger. Kind of a big deal. The mayor's making an appearance." He picked up his bags of bread, thanking Betsy.

Lucy was surprised. "Really? When did that come about?" She'd just talked to Taylor last night and he hadn't mentioned it.

Taylor drained the last of his coffee, setting the cup down. "Oh, it's been in the works for a while now. The department even sponsored an art contest with the kids on how to stay safe in public. Should be fun to see what they've come up with."

"That sounds neat!" Betsy chimed in, and Lucy nodded. *It did sound neat. But why hadn't Taylor mentioned it to her sooner?*

"Well, have fun!" Lucy called, as Taylor shouldered his way through the door.

He grinned, saying, "I'll call you tonight!"

The bell jangled, and he was gone. Lucy felt a niggling sense of dissatisfaction with their brief visit. First, Taylor hadn't seemed to have much compassion for Daphne… and then this, a very important day for him, and he'd not said a word about it beforehand.

Pensively, Lucy wiped at a spot on the glass of the pastry case, while Betsy picked up her pen and the magazine, completing the magazine quiz in silence. Lucy was privately thankful Betsy had stopped reading the questions out loud.

"Would you look at that!" Betsy crowed, setting her pen down. "Ninety-eight points out of a hundred!" She recited the result.

"The two of you are like two peas in a pod—soulmates whose compatibility transcends time. Go pick out a white dress!"

Betsy chuckled, her cheeks pink. She was obviously tickled with the result. She looked over at Lucy, her eyes sparkling. "If you don't mind, I'll take my lunch break now. I want to call Joseph and see how his day's going."

At Lucy's nod, Betsy snagged an espresso-chip muffin and a latte and headed for the staircase. "I'll be upstairs in the office," she called out.

Lucy straightened the pastry trays in the case, erased the morning specials from the chalkboard, and fiddled with the arrangement of local honey, all the while very aware of the magazine laying on the counter. Finally, unable to resist, she flipped it back open to the quiz and grabbed a pen.

Jotting down her answers on a napkin, she tried to answer each question honestly, while reminding herself the whole thing was just for her own amusement, and not to take it too seriously.

Work or play oriented? Solitary or people-lover? Cat lover, dog lover, or no pets?

The list went on, and Lucy continued doggedly until each question was answered, then tallied up her score.

48 out of 100.

She stared down at the figure. *That can't be good.* She quickly re-added the score, but it came out the same. With a sigh, she flipped to the results section.

"Although they say opposites attract, remember, oil and water don't mix. With such vastly different personalities, it might be time to cut your losses before you waste any more time. But don't be blue—there are plenty of fish in the sea."

Dismayed, Lucy stared at the words for a long moment before abruptly flipping the magazine shut and pushing it away.

She wished she'd never taken the silly quiz.

5

When her alarm beeped the next morning, Lucy was sorely tempted to shut it off and go back to sleep. She'd slept fitfully last night, tossing and turning with the questions from the quiz running through her mind. Even though she knew it was just a bit of fluff in a women's magazine, it still stung to read the results.

It hadn't helped the situation when Taylor had neglected to call her last night. She knew he'd probably just been busy or caught up in something and not realized the time until late. But she sure would have liked to have heard his voice, just to reassure herself that they were a solid couple, no matter what some stupid quiz said.

Lucy lay there, staring listlessly at the ceiling, until Gigi hopped on the bed to investigate. Gigi was her beloved white Persian, and as always, she managed to bring a smile to Lucy's face.

Gigi head-butted Lucy's hand, as if to say, *hey, why aren't you petting me?* A rumbling purr sounded as Lucy caressed the animal's soft fur, taking comfort in Gigi's companionship. The feline was content for a moment, then emitted a squeaky meow, jumping off the bed and trotting to the door. She turned and looked back at Lucy expectantly.

Lucy groaned and rolled out of bed, wrapping herself in a robe. "Yes, yes, it's breakfast time," she said, yawning and stepping into her slippers. Gigi sashayed out to the kitchen to wait.

A few minutes later, Lucy walked into the homey kitchen, where Aunt Tricia was already seated at their small table. Bright winter sunshine streamed in through the white linen curtains embroidered with blue flowers.

This kitchen was Lucy's favorite room in the house. She could almost envision her mother standing there, cooking breakfast at the stove, as she'd done almost every morning of Lucy's childhood. It had always been just the three of them; Lucy, her mother, and her father, and their life revolved around Sweet Delights Bakery, which Lucy's parents had opened together.

Lucy had taken the bakery for granted her whole childhood, envisioning herself leaving Ivy Creek behind for the big city and never looking back. But sometimes the reality of our dreams is very different than we'd imagined, and life in the city, working as a professional food blogger, had left Lucy feeling as if something indefinable was missing from her life.

It wasn't until tragedy struck that Lucy realized Ivy Creek, with its small-town lifestyle, was what she'd been pining for. When Lucy's parents were killed in an accident, she'd returned to Ivy Creek to settle their estate, and found herself not wanting to leave.

Instead of selling the house and bakery, as she'd intended, Lucy decided to run the bakery herself, with the help of her aunt. She invited Aunt Tricia to come and live with her in her childhood home, and everything had just fallen into place. She'd never once looked back.

"Good morning," Aunt Tricia greeted her, buttering a slice of toast. She had a newspaper folded open to the crossword puzzle, half filled in already.

"Morning," Lucy poured herself a cup of coffee, seriously needing a caffeine boost. Gigi meowed, tapping Lucy's leg to remind her she hadn't been fed yet. With a sigh, Lucy set her mug on the counter and reached into the cabinet for the bag of dry cat food.

"There you go, princess," she said, measuring out a portion. Gigi swished her tail and immediately busied herself at her dish, while Lucy grabbed her cup and sank into a chair.

Aunt Tricia looked at Lucy over the top of her glasses. "Busy day, today?"

Lucy nodded. She loved how successful the bakery had become under her care, but there were some days she wished for a little more breathing space. Like today…

"Besides the usual stocking up, we have eight cakes to decorate, three cupcake orders, and we need to finish decorating the cookie-gram samples."

Lucy had told Aunt Tricia about the cookie-gram idea last night, and her aunt had thoroughly supported it, suggesting Lucy put up flyers at the college to advertise her new product.

Aunt Tricia smiled, a faraway look in her eyes. "I remember the first time your uncle gave me a Valentine's Day card. I was sixteen, and he was seventeen. He was quite an artist, you know. He drew it himself, and all my girlfriends were jealous."

Lucy smiled, having heard the story many times. "I bet they were." The soul mate compatibility quiz popped back into her head, again, and she tried to banish it. "Did you know right away you wanted to marry him?"

Aunt Tricia shook her head, a mischievous look in her eyes. "No, although he repeatedly told me we were destined to be together! I had never seen myself as the marrying type. My head was too full of dreams of travel and adventure." She arched an eyebrow at Lucy.

"Little did I know, adventures are twice as enjoyable when you're with someone special." She took a sip of coffee, then set her cup down. "Perhaps you and Taylor should take a short vacation in the spring. You both work so hard all the time."

Lucy opened her mouth to answer, but before she could, the telephone rang.

"Saved by the bell," she joked, getting up from the table. She wondered if it could be Taylor, since he'd neglected to call last night. It was rather early for anyone else to call.

She picked up the receiver. "Hello?"

An unfamiliar masculine voice greeted her. "Hi, Lucy. I apologize for the hour, but I wanted to catch you before you got to the bakery."

Lucy frowned, unable to place the caller. "I'm sorry... who is this?"

A small chuckle. "Sorry, I should have led with that. It's Miles Clifton. Joseph gave me your number. I hope that's OK."

Lucy assured him, "Oh, of course! What can I do for you, Miles?"

Miles hesitated, then said, "Betsy was telling us about your new product – the Valentine's Day cookie-gram. By the way, she's already got a couple of students who agreed to be delivery persons, in exchange for bakery credit." He chuckled. "I can't say I blame them! I almost volunteered myself."

Lucy smiled. She had a feeling she knew what Miles was going to say next.

He continued, "So, I'd like to order one, please. But I want it to be a secret, if you can find a way to do it all yourself. I'd like it to be chocolate, on Betsy's advice."

Lucy glanced at Aunt Tricia and found her watching Lucy quizzically. Lucy winked at her and asked Miles, "Chocolate. Got it. And it's for…?"

Miles answered, confirming Lucy's suspicion, and her heart did a happy dance in her chest.

"It's for Hannah. I'd like for it to be delivered to her house this evening, if that's possible."

Lucy assured him. "Oh, yes, not a problem. What would you like it to say?"

Miles cleared his throat, sounding a little embarrassed.

"Sweets for the sweet. Dinner together? Signed Miles"

Lucy grinned, writing down the inscription. "Got it."

"Is that too much writing?" Miles asked nervously.

Lucy assured him, "Nope. It's perfect. We'll get it delivered to Hannah's place this evening."

As she hung up the phone, Lucy briefly closed her eyes, casting a fervent wish into the universe.

Please, please, let Hannah accept his invitation and give Miles a chance.

She wasn't sure why, but she had a feeling Miles and Hannah may be kindred spirits.

6

Lucy glanced at the clock in the kitchen and then looked over to see what Hannah was doing. She needed to get Miles' cookie-gram decorated so the icing would dry by this afternoon. Baking it secretly had not been a problem, as she and Hannah were involved in different tasks, but she really didn't want to chance Hannah seeing her write out the message.

Betsy saved the day, appearing in the archway connecting the kitchen to the front. Her eyes met Lucy's, and Lucy tilted her head toward Hannah, trying to communicate her wishes.

Betsy caught Lucy's intentions and spoke up. "Hannah, I know you already told me once this morning, but I'm afraid I keep mixing up which flavor is which, on the puff pastry turnovers. If you have a second, could you come out front and tell me again? I'll make a cheat sheet this time, I promise."

Hannah grumbled good-naturedly but laid her tools down and followed Betsy out front. Lucy moved quickly, grabbing the pastry bag of royal icing, and retrieving the chocolate cookie-gram from where she'd stashed it. With a skill born of years of practice, she piped a swirling border in white, added pink and red hearts, and carefully printed out the message from Miles.

Quickly popping the cookie-gram into a box, she had just closed the lid and was carrying it over to the finished product rack when Hannah walked back into the kitchen with Betsy.

Betsy veered off to intercept Lucy, taking the box from her hands.

"I'll just bring this out front," she said, her blue eyes merry. Lucy tried to tamp down her conspiratorial grin before Hannah got suspicious.

Now that her part of the scheme was done, Lucy relaxed into her regular schedule, decorating the cakes and cupcakes ordered for the day, while crossing her fingers that Hannah would give Miles a chance.

IT WAS EARLY the next morning, and Lucy, Aunt Tricia, and Betsy sat huddled together at their favorite table in the bakery. An air of worry hung over the group like a cloud. Hannah had not arrived yet, which was very out of character - she was habitually early.

Betsy confirmed that the delivery boy had indeed handed the boxed cookie-gram directly to Hannah at six o'clock last night. Lucy was wondering if they'd made a huge mistake, interfering in Hannah's personal life. She would have expected Hannah to telephone her, upon receiving the cookie-gram, but she hadn't.

Was she irritated? Was Miles going to be rejected?

"Should we call her?" asked Betsy, her eyes full of concern as she dipped a chocolate biscotti in her coffee.

Lucy shook her head. "She's not late yet. She's just not early."

Suddenly, they heard the kitchen's back door open and shut. Footsteps sounded from that direction. The ladies' heads swiveled as one to see Hannah appearing in the archway, unwinding a scarf from her neck.

"Sorry I'm late," she called out, hanging up her coat and scarf.

"You're not late," Lucy assured her, studying her friend's face for a sign of... something.

Hannah looked surprised. "I'm not? It feels like I am."

She poured herself a coffee and wandered over to their table, taking a seat. Taking a sip, she set the cup down and looked around at the three of them.

"So, what's on for today?" she asked casually, her expression blank.

She was met with silence. Looking at the three women's identical, puzzled expressions, she burst out laughing.

"You guys should see your faces," she chortled, her eyes gleaming. "Yes, I received the cookie-gram! And yes. I called Miles and accepted his invitation." She grinned and sipped her coffee, looking amused.

"Yay!" exclaimed Betsy, clapping her hands with delight, like a child.

Lucy and Aunt Tricia exchanged smiles, and Lucy asked, "So? When? And where?"

"Sizzle. This weekend," Hannah confirmed. "And I hope you don't mind, Lucy, but since I knew you and Taylor were already going, I suggested we double-date." She turned hopeful eyes on Lucy, and Lucy nodded, pleased at the idea.

"Sure! It'll be fun!"

Hannah sighed with relief. "Good. Because to be honest, I'm a little nervous. It'll be a lot easier if it's not just me and Miles." She looked at Betsy and Aunt Tricia. "We can make it one big outing, if you guys want to go."

Aunt Tricia smiled, but declined, and Betsy shook her head. "Joseph and I are going there for our Valentine's date night next Friday. But thank you."

Lucy glanced at her watch and stood up. "OK, my friends, five minutes to opening."

The ladies all got up and began their morning duties, with Aunt Tricia stocking the cash register, Hannah taking inventory of the pastries, and Betsy prepping the coffee machines, while Lucy wrote the morning's specials on the chalkboard.

About an hour after opening, Lucy and Hannah were standing in front of the pastry case, debating on switching out cheesecake bars for pralines, when the bell jangled.

A cheery voice called out. "Good morning, ladies!"

Lucy turned to see Daphne Bell, Bert Dobbin's ex-girlfriend, entering the bakery. Daphne ran the local animal shelter, and Lucy had met her several times before. She knew Daphne as a very loving, sweet, individual, and she wondered how the woman was handling her sudden notoriety after the failed public proposal.

"Daphne, hi!" Lucy greeted her. "So good to see you!"

Betsy and Aunt Tricia added their hellos, but Lucy noticed Hannah did not speak, though she smiled in welcome.

"Hannah, have you met Daphne?" Lucy asked, surprised that the ladies didn't seem to know each other.

Both women shook their heads, and Lucy made the introductions.

"Daphne runs the animal shelter at the edge of town," Lucy informed Hannah, knowing Hannah would admire the woman's vocation.

"Oh, wow, that's great!" Hannah said, smiling at Daphne. "It's my dream to someday run a shelter from my house."

Daphne grinned, her bright green eyes a vivid contrast to her dark hair. "Dogs or cats?"

Hannah chuckled. "Both, preferably. As long as they get along."

"Well, if you ever want to get your feet wet, we have a program where folks can foster stray dogs and cats while they wait for adoption," Daphne said.

Hannah looked surprised. "Oh! Is Miles Clifton one of your foster parents? I know he's doing that right now, for dogs, but I'm not sure what shelter he's involved with."

Daphne nodded. "Yes, he is!" A wide smile broke across her face. "Miles is the best! He also helps out when he can with some shelter responsibilities. We really rely on our volunteers." She looked at Hannah quizzically. "Do you know him well? I thought he was pretty new to town."

Hannah's cheeks turned pink, and a soft smile crept over her features. "Ah, no… not yet anyway… but…"

Betsy piped up. "Miles is taking Hannah out to dinner this weekend!"

Daphne looked delighted. "So, you're the girl he's been mooning over!" She chuckled as Hannah turned redder, still. "Aw, that's so sweet. I hope you guys have a wonderful time."

She turned to Lucy next. "Speaking of the shelter, I'm hoping to buy some of Lenora Nelson's dog biscuits. Do you have plenty available? I need twenty-five."

"I sure do." Lucy led Daphne over to Mrs. Nelson's small vendor table, piled high with bags of homemade dog cookies from Nelson Farms. It was a new product, and they were selling very well.

Daphne studied several labels before choosing three different bags. "These look great," she commented. "Do you know if she ever makes cat treats?"

Lucy shook her head. "Not that I've heard of, but I'll mention it to her when she comes in next."

Daphne brought her selection over to the counter, and Betsy rang her up.

Daphne cleared her throat, speaking softly. "Betsy… I hope I didn't ruin opening night, but I… I just couldn't…" She struggled with the words.

Betsy's face softened as she waved away Daphne's concerns. "No, of course you didn't. You didn't do anything wrong, Daphne. I'm sorry it all went down that way."

Daphne sighed. "Me too." She didn't seem to want to talk about it further, and Lucy was glad Betsy let it drop.

Daphne gathered up her purchases and turned to leave the bakery, looking back over her shoulder as she called to the ladies.

"Thank you and have a wonderful day! And Hannah, it was so nice to meet you!"

As Daphne reached the entrance, she turned to face forward, running smack into the man coming through the door.

Bert Dobbins.

7

Lucy watched, cringing for both parties as their obvious discomfort was plain to see.

"Ah, excuse me, Bert." Daphne seemed anxious as she looked into her ex-lover's face. "Are you… is everything OK?"

Bert looked miserable, his eyes shadowed and heartbroken. He nodded stiffly and stepped aside. "Sure," he said, refusing to meet Daphne's eyes.

Daphne hesitated just a moment, then nodded and hurried past him, exiting the bakery without another word.

Even after she'd left, the tension in the room was palpable. Bert stood facing the front counter, his eyes unseeing, his shoulders slumped. He seemed to be rooted to the spot.

"Hey, Bert!" Lucy called out, trying to sound cheerful. "I heard you're the best Romeo this town has ever seen."

She'd meant to be supportive, but given the circumstances, the words sounded a bit inappropriate, and she tried to think of something to add.

Hannah saved the day. "Just the man I wanted to see! Aren't you working at Sizzle restaurant now?"

Bert's eyes focused on Hannah, and slowly he nodded, coming out of his trance. He stepped over to the counter. "Hi, Hannah. Yes, I am. Have you come by yet?"

Hannah shook her head. "Not yet, but four of us are going this weekend. What would you recommend?"

Bert's background as a seasoned cook took over. He fell naturally into kitchen talk, one culinary professional to another, advising Hannah on what Sizzle's best entrees were.

"What's all this fuss about your marinade?" Hannah asked. "Is it really that good?"

Bert smiled slightly. "It's not my marinade. It's Oliver Crenshaw's recipe, though I'm the one who mixes it up. And I tell you, it *is* that good. It's even better than Wrigley's."

His tone was proud, and Lucy was glad Hannah had been able to bring him out of his shock over seeing Daphne.

"We're really looking forward to it," Lucy chimed in, and Aunt Tricia added her two cents.

"It's about time Wrigley's had a little competition." Her tone was disapproving. "In my opinion, Lionel Wrigley has never treated his employees very well. Maybe he'll change his ways now that he's not the only game in town."

Bert nodded, his lips thinning. "I can vouch for that. I did a stint at Wrigley's myself. The only employee Wrigley cares about is Chef Fugasi. The rest of his crew means nothing to him. He treats them all like dirt."

Bert stopped talking as his eyes roamed over the pastry selection. His expression brightened, spotting the raspberry-coconut jelly roll slices in the glass case.

"Oh, great! That's exactly what I came in for. Could I have two of those jelly roll slices, please, and a large coffee with cream and sugar, to go."

Betsy filled his order, and the two of them exchanged a few words about the play before Bert paid for his purchase and picked up his bag and to-go cup.

"Well, I guess I'll see you guys at Sizzle," he called out to Hannah as he turned to go.

The ladies said their goodbyes, and the bell jangled as he exited the bakery.

"Whew!" Hannah said. "That was pretty intense with Daphne and Bert."

Betsy nodded. "It's so sad. I guess it's going to take time before they're comfortable with each other again."

Aunt Tricia took off her glasses, cleaning the lenses with a napkin. "I think it's a good thing Bert's keeping busy. Working at Sizzle might be the best thing to take his mind off the breakup, since the restaurant's become so popular, so fast."

Lucy nodded, her thoughts drifting to their upcoming double date. For Hannah's sake, she hoped everything would go perfectly.

"I can't go," Hannah declared. "I feel sick." She slumped down on the couch.

Lucy shook her head, taking her friend by the arms and standing her back up. "You're fine. You're just nervous."

The girls were at Lucy's house, waiting for Taylor and Miles to pick them up. Going in one vehicle had been Lucy's idea, thinking it would ease Hannah's nerves a little to not have to travel alone with Miles. At this point, she was glad of that decision, because left on her own, Hannah might well have canceled at the last minute.

Lucy studied her friend's face, wondering why she was so anxious. "What gives, Hannah? I've never seen you so nervous about a guy. It's just a dinner date."

Hannah was quiet for a minute. When she looked up, the naked apprehension in her eyes pained Lucy's heart.

"I just really like him," Hannah confessed softly. "I'm afraid I'm going to mess it up. It seems... important, for some reason."

Lucy spoke firmly. "You're not going to mess anything up. You're going to have a wonderful time. I have a good feeling about this, Hannah. You guys have a lot in common."

Aunt Tricia called out from the other room that the guys had arrived, and Lucy caught Hannah's eye.

"Ready?"

Hannah took a deep breath and nodded. "Ready. Bring on the steak!"

Lucy chuckled. "That's the spirit!"

The drive over was uneventful, with Taylor driving and Hannah and Miles riding in the back. Lucy could hear light banter between the pair and smiled to herself.

Hannah seemed to be over her cold feet.

They pulled into the restaurant parking lot, and Lucy was surprised at how many cars there were already. And here she'd thought they'd timed it well, before the dinner rush. She turned to Taylor.

"Uh-oh. Do you think we should have made a reservation?"

He shrugged. "Maybe. But we're here now, for better or for worse. Let's see how long the wait time is."

The foursome disembarked and made their way up the flagstone walkway. Sizzle Restaurant had an impressive appearance, with a natural stone exterior and tinted glass windows. As they approached the entrance, Lucy could see several people sitting in the lobby.

Taylor held the door as the group entered and tried to find a spot to stand out of the way.

"I'll go see how long the wait is," Taylor said, stepping over to the hostess station.

Miles turned to Hannah. "I'm sorry. I should have thought about how popular this place was and made us a reservation ahead of time."

Hannah smiled, seeming to be completely at ease in his company. "It's OK. I'm not in a rush. If it's going to be awhile, we can always wait at the bar."

Taylor reappeared, relief evident in his expression. "It's not as bad as it looks. Ten minutes, they said."

Even as he spoke, a party of six that had been waiting stood and followed the hostess into the dining area. Lucy, Hannah, Miles, and Taylor sat down on the bench the group had occupied, and Lucy loosened her coat. The aroma drifting out from the kitchen was heavenly.

Hannah nudged her. "Look over there. Do you know who that is?" Her tone was hushed.

Lucy looked to where Hannah nodded with her chin and saw a portly fellow with graying hair and bushy eyebrows, who looked to be in his early fifties. He stood next to the hostess station with his face set in a scowl. His arms were folded, and he tapped his foot, conveying his impatience.

Lucy frowned, thinking she should recognize the man, but couldn't quite place him.

"No. Who is it?"

Taylor had caught wind of their conversation and turned to look, as well. He answered Lucy's question himself, with surprise in his tone.

"That's Chef Fugasi, from Wrigley's Steakhouse. I wonder what he's doing here?"

8

"Hmm," Lucy studied the man, who now seemed to be arguing with the hostess.

The harried woman kept a pleasant expression pasted on her face, though the chef grew increasingly irate, his complexion turning a mottled red, and his bushy brows dipping lower over his eyes.

As Lucy's group watched, another employee approached and spoke briefly to the hostess, then led Chef Fugasi away, presumably to be seated.

"Wow, he doesn't seem very nice," Hannah observed. "I've heard stories he was difficult to work under."

"I bet he's here to check out Sizzle's marinade," Lucy speculated. "If anyone could tell if it was the exact same recipe or just similar, it would be a seasoned chef."

"How could Oliver Crenshaw have stolen Wrigley's marinade recipe, anyway?" Taylor asked, frowning. "From what I've heard, it's a closely guarded secret."

"Maybe a disgruntled employee who used to work at Wrigley's?" suggested Miles. "Wouldn't they have access?"

Lucy shook her head. "Not according to Bert Dobbins. He worked at Wrigley's before working here, and he said Chef Fugasi was the only one allowed near the recipe."

Their conversation halted as the hostess appeared, telling them their table was ready. The group followed her into the artfully decorated dining room, where wall sconces glowed softly against burgundy painted walls accented with oak wainscoting.

The men held the chairs for the ladies, and the four settled into their table, ordering a bottle of red wine.

Lucy looked around appreciatively. Oliver Crenshaw must have hired a really great designer, she thought. The atmosphere was comfortable and subdued, with the rich tones of red and brown offering warmth and welcome, while hints of gold accents conveyed understated luxury.

"Very nice," Hannah said, looking around as well. She glanced over at Miles with a grin. "Points for you on destination."

Miles chuckled, his green eyes crinkling. "I'm glad you approve. I've heard great things about this place."

Lucy's eyes roamed over the patrons, finding the chef seated in the center of the dining room, with the same frown plastered over his features. He snapped his fingers at a passing waitress, who glanced over her shoulder at him, narrowing her eyes.

"Uh-oh," Hannah said in a low tone. "Maybe some bad blood there."

Lucy looked at her with surprise. "Why do you say that?"

Hannah indicated the young waitress with a nod. "That's Mandy Taft. She used to work at Wrigley's. They don't look like they like each other."

Lucy observed the pair, concluding Hannah was right.

Mandy's lips were thinned as she jotted down the chef's order, and her posture conveyed her irritation. She snapped the pad shut and walked a few steps away, pausing as the chef spoke once more from behind her. In two strides she was at his table again, her eyes flashing in anger as she leaned in close, saying something meant for his ears, alone.

Chef Fugasi drew back, his expression conveying shock and contempt, and Mandy spun on her heel, walking away. The chef stared after her with his eyes narrowed, reaching for his wine glass.

"Wow, you're not kidding," Taylor commented, having witnessed the scene. "I wonder what she said to him?"

Their wine arrived at that moment, and conversation ceased as glasses were poured. When the waitress began to pour a glass for Miles, he smiled but indicated a pass, sipping from his water glass. Observing this, something occurred to Lucy. She glanced at Hannah speculatively, but found her friend distracted by a solitary figure, eating alone at a corner table.

"Hey, isn't that Dr. Jax?" Hannah nodded in the man's direction.

Dr. Jax was the town veterinarian. His loving care of all the four-legged residents in Ivy Creek made him a very popular man. He was only in his mid-thirties but was seven years a widower, having lost his wife to cancer only two years after they'd been married. Lucy hadn't been living in Ivy Creek at the time, but she remembered Aunt Tricia telling her about the poor man's tragic loss.

The man looked up suddenly, and Lucy saw Hannah was right. "Hi, Dr. Jax!" Lucy called out and waved.

A smile broke out on the man's face as he recognized their group, and he pushed away from his table, coming over to say hello.

"Well, what do we have here? Some of Ivy Creek's finest citizens, all at one table," he greeted them, his face lighting up with a genuine smile.

Lucy grinned back. With thinning brown hair and nondescript features, Dr. Jax's average looks were elevated by his infectious smile.

"Dr. Jax, great to see you!" Hannah said. She indicated Miles. "I'd like you to meet Miles Clifton. He's new in town."

Dr. Jax winked at Miles. "Miles and I are acquainted," he told Hannah, who looked surprised. Addressing Miles, Dr. Jax raised an eyebrow humorously, "You're keeping some pretty good company tonight."

Miles laughed. "Yes, sir, without a doubt." He turned to Hannah. "Dr. Jax is over at Daphne's animal shelter quite a bit, and I volunteer there when I can."

Dr. Jax nodded. "Miles is one of our best volunteers. If only more residents would step up like he has, in just the few months he's been in town, we'd have much less of a stray animal problem."

Hannah looked at Miles with admiration in her eyes. "I wish I could take in more strays, but my cat Spooky is all I can handle at the moment."

Lucy spoke up. "So, Dr. Jax, this is our first time eating here. Have you been to Sizzle before?"

Dr. Jax's eyes twinkled. "I am officially a regular customer. I worked out a barter system with the owner, Mr. Crenshaw. He has two dalmatians, one of whom has a condition that needs to be monitored regularly. So, to lessen his cost, I have dinner here twice a week." He grinned. "You're in for a real treat! The food is fantastic."

Taylor addressed the man, his tone serious. "Doctor J, have you had any more disturbances at your house?"

Seeing the looks of concern exchanged around the table, Dr. Jax clarified. "I had a prowler set off my alarm system last night, and I had to call the station. Thankfully, the siren scared him away."

He shook his head, answering Taylor. "Nothing damaged or taken. I did a walk around the property this morning."

Taylor pursed his lips, his brows drawing together. "And you couldn't see any identifying details about the man?"

Dr. Jax sighed. "No, unfortunately, one of the spotlights at the side of the house was out. I just caught a glimpse of a figure dressed in black. Not overly large or small, I'd say. Average height."

Lucy frowned, turning to Taylor. "Do we need to be worried? Have there been any more reports like that coming in across town?"

Taylor settled his arm over her shoulders. "Nothing for you to worry about, honey. Just an isolated incident. Might have been some out-of-towner, looking for a quick smash and grab."

Lucy nodded, reassured by his words. She didn't have an alarm system on her house, although in recent years, she'd been considering it.

Dr. Jax glanced back at his table. "Well, it was nice to see you all, but I should finish up my dinner. It's so busy here tonight, I'm sure seating is at a premium."

With a mock salute, the veterinarian turned away to a chorus of goodbyes.

As he settled back into his chair, Lucy's thoughts circled back to the conversation.

A quick smash and grab? With Dr. Jax's car in the driveway and his lights on in the house?

That didn't seem likely.

9

"Wow, I don't like the sound of that," Hannah remarked. "I'm so glad Dr. Jax didn't have to confront the prowler inside his home." She sipped her wine, then noticed Miles didn't have a glass.

"Oh. Wine, Miles?" she asked, setting her glass down and reaching for the bottle.

Miles shook his head with a smile. "I don't drink alcohol," he explained. "Just a personal choice."

Hannah's eyebrows raised. "Ohhh..." she drew the word out, her brow wrinkling. She cocked her head, musing out loud. "So... New Year's Eve..."

Miles nodded his head. His smile turning wry. "Yes, that was why I declined your invitation. I really should have explained."

Lucy grinned as she watched Hannah process that information. Her friend's self-confidence was coming back, and this tidbit of news was like the cherry on top. Miles had not declined a date with her, he'd declined a drink with her. A big difference.

"Well, we can have a toast anyway," Taylor announced. He raised his glass, looking at Lucy. "To love," he said with a wink.

Lucy smiled warmly at him, then lifted her glass. "To love… and to new friendships!"

Miles lifted his water glass. "To new beginnings," he said, looking at Hannah. Her cheeks pinked, but she smiled radiantly.

"To…" Hannah held her glass up and they all looked at her, waiting expectantly. "Steak!" She concluded her toast with a grin, and laughter was heard around the table. "Seriously, folks, I'm starving."

They perused the menus, deciding to split a few entrees so they could sample more. Mandy took their order, her cheerful expression and professional attitude a major contrast to her interactions with Chef Fugasi. She collected their menus and promised to bring their appetizers out in a jiffy.

Taylor looked around, admiring the gleaming woodwork. "Pretty classy place," he commented. "I bet Crenshaw will do well here."

Lucy murmured her agreement, and turned to Miles, unable to squelch her natural curiosity any longer. "So, Miles, where are you from originally?"

Miles turned his gold-flecked green eyes on her, his expression relaxed and friendly. "New Hampshire," he offered. "Franconia Notch area."

"New Hampshire," Hannah commented, nodding her head. "Nice! So, you're no stranger to snow, then."

"I love snow!" Miles announced in an overly bright voice, before laughing and shaking his head. "Not!"

Hannah twisted around to look at him, confused. "So, you *don't* like snow?" she clarified, her face a bit hopeful. Hannah detested the snow, Lucy knew. Her friend bemoaned the white stuff every winter.

Miles shook his head with an expression of distaste. "Wet. Cold. Messy roads. Muddy paws… what's there to like?" he glanced at Hannah's face. "How about you?"

Hannah grinned at him. "I hate the stuff. I'd move somewhere that didn't have it, but… ha. Well, my whole life is here," she admitted. She took a sip of wine. "And Colorado is pretty nice, anyway," she conceded.

"Colorado is very nice," Miles agreed, studying Hannah's face. "A lovely place, indeed."

Hannah blushed and took a sip of water. "How did you become involved in animal rescue?" she asked. "Was it something you did in New Hampshire as well?"

Miles nodded. "My mom ran a cat shelter out of the heated barn on our property while I was growing up. And we always had dogs as pets, so I got pretty used to being around both of them, cats and dogs."

"That's so cool," Lucy commented admiringly. "How many cats did your mom take care of?"

Miles chuckled. "Sometimes just three or four. It depended how quickly she could find homes for them. One time we had fourteen."

"Fourteen!" Taylor exclaimed. "That's a lot of kibble."

Mandy appeared with their appetizers just then, and Lucy and Hannah scooted their glasses to the edge of the table to make room.

"Is your family still living in New Hampshire?" Hannah asked. "Your mom sounds like my kind of person." She dipped a mozzarella stick in marinara sauce.

Miles shook his head. "I lost my mother last May," he said, in a quiet tone. It was clear the grief was still fresh. "I have two brothers, but we're all kind of spread across the country now. We still own the land in New Hampshire, but we'll probably wind up selling it."

The mood at the table turned solemn as the others offered their condolences. Lucy tried to steer them to a cheerier conversation.

"I just have one pet, a Persian cat named Gigi. She's a handful, but I admit, it's crossed my mind now and then that she might like a companion."

"Two Gigis?" Taylor echoed in mock horror, and Lucy giggled, elbowing him. She spooned some spinach artichoke dip onto a piece of French bread.

"I can't imagine having only one pet forever." She studied Taylor's familiar face. "How about you, Taylor? A dog person? A cat person? Or both?" Lucy asked the question casually, ignoring the little voice in her head that reminded her that the same question had been posed on the soul mate compatibility quiz.

"Definitely dogs over cats," Taylor replied, and Lucy blinked, but kept her face expressionless. "Ideally, two dogs. More than two couldn't fit on the bed."

Lucy stared at him. "Dogs on the bed? The people bed?"

Taylor raised his eyebrows. "Gigi sleeps on your bed," he pointed out.

Lucy protested. "But Gigi is clean. Extremely clean, she's spotlessly white."

Hannah changed the subject, seeing Lucy's face. "I think it would be very rewarding to run an animal shelter," she commented. "I'd love to come out and take a look at Daphne's shelter, see all the ins and outs."

Miles grinned with genuine pleasure. "Let's go together. I'd love to show you around. Maybe next week?" He popped a fried mushroom into his mouth.

Hannah nodded her head enthusiastically. "It's a plan!"

The clang of silverware being dropped forcefully on porcelain rang out from the center of the dining room. Startled, Lucy turned her head to see Chef Fugasi push his chair away from his small table and stand abruptly, his face contorted with anger.

"Thief!" he shouted, waving his arms at the ceiling. His face was beet red as he swiveled his head to address the shocked patrons of Sizzle Restaurant. "Oliver Crenshaw is a thief!"

Fugasi snatched up his fork, spearing the cut slab of steak from his plate. He held the meat aloft, waggling it as evidence before a jury.

"This marinade recipe was stolen! For many years, I made this marinade every day, and I tell you, this is Wrigley's secret formula, stolen by Sizzle Restaurant! Thief! Thief!" he bellowed, his bushy gray eyebrows drawn together.

10

The wait staff looked horrified, unsure of what to do. The other patrons had paused, frozen, some with forks halfway to their mouths, watching the scene play out like a train crash.

"Thief!" Chef Fugasi cried again, looking around the dining room. He seemed to relish having an audience.

Taylor frowned and pushed his chair away from their table, rising to his feet. Lucy watched as he walked over to stand next to the irate man, speaking quietly, but with authority.

"Chef Fugasi, I'm going to have to ask you to calm down."

The chef turned to view Taylor with an incredulous expression. "Calm down? Calm down? A crime has been committed here! Arrest Oliver Crenshaw! The man is a thief!"

He waved his fork in the air for emphasis, and Lucy watched the speared steak wobble, wondering if it might wind up on the floor or possibly sail through the air to another patron's table.

Taylor's tone was low but firm. "This is Mr. Crenshaw's place of business, Chef Fugasi. I can't let you interfere with a man's livelihood. If you, or Mr. Wrigley, want to contest the origin of the marinade recipe, it will have to be done in a court of law. Not here."

Chef Fugasi pointedly ignored him, looking away and bellowing, "I want justice! A crime has been committed!"

Taylor narrowed his eyes and clamped a strong hand down on the chef's shoulder. His voice became more forceful. "Sir, please sit down and finish your meal, or leave the premises, so the rest of us can enjoy ours."

Chef Fugasi turned his head and glared at Taylor. He threw his fork back down on the table with a clatter.

"You have not heard the end of this!" he bellowed at the ceiling, threatening the establishment at large. He stomped out of the dining room, leaving the other patrons looking after him with shocked expressions.

Silence hung over the room for a few seconds before the buzz of conversation began again. Mandy appeared to clear the chef's table and Taylor returned to his seat, looking annoyed.

"Sorry about that," he said, and took a restorative sip of wine. He shook his head, setting his glass down. "Looks like Crenshaw has a battle ahead of him."

Miles nodded. "That was one angry man. I don't believe he's going to let the matter go."

"Do you think they'll really try to sue Mr. Crenshaw over a recipe?" Lucy asked, her eyes wide.

Hannah pursed her lips. "Copyright law in regard to recipes is a tricky thing," she pointed out. "All you have to do is change two ingredients, and it's no longer considered the same recipe."

"Beyond that, I don't think Fugasi, or Wrigley could convince a judge that someone got their hands on a closely guarded family recipe," Taylor said. "How would they ever prove it?"

Mandy appeared at that moment, with sizzling plates of steak and chicken.

"So sorry for that disturbance, folks," she murmured, setting their entrees down. "Ketchup for your fries?"

"Mustard, please," Hannah and Miles said in unison. They looked at each other, surprised.

"Mustard on French fries?" Hannah clarified, with an eyebrow raised.

Miles grinned. "Always."

Hannah chuckled and nodded. "It is clearly superior," she agreed.

Lucy hid a smile. Even with the unwelcome disturbance, she could see tonight was the beginning of something good for Hannah.

Taylor cut a piece of his steak and sampled it. "Oh, yes," he praised, chewing with his eyes closed.

"That good?" Lucy tried a bite herself. It was heavenly. "Mmm…"

Hannah swallowed a forkful and agreed wholeheartedly. "OK, yes, this has got to be the best marinade I've ever tasted."

"But is it Wrigley's recipe?" Lucy asked in a low tone, half-joking.

Hannah shrugged. "It's been so long since I've been to Wrigley's I can't even tell you if it's similar," she admitted. "And with Chef Fugasi's little display, I'm not really inclined to bop on over there to check for myself. I like this place better."

Miles nodded, digging into his meal. "I think this might be my new favorite restaurant."

Hannah chuckled. "Are you going to be a regular, like Dr. Jax?"

Miles grinned. "Maybe. You want to be a regular with me? Pick a day, and we'll make it a standing dinner date."

Hannah looked pleased. "I will take that under serious consideration," she promised.

Taylor bumped Lucy's knee under the table with his own. As she glanced up at him, he cut his eyes at Hannah and Miles and waggled his eyebrows. Lucy smiled and looked back down, focusing on her meal with gladness in her heart. It was about time Hannah found someone to spend time with.

Lucy looked up and around the room, seeing that the patrons had gone back to eating, the chef's outburst all but forgotten. As her gaze fell on the entrance to the kitchen, she saw a familiar figure come through the double doors.

It was Oliver Crenshaw. She watched as he began to make the rounds, stopping at each table to exchange a few words with his customers.

"Here's the man himself," Lucy commented, nodding with her chin. "That's Mr. Crenshaw, over there."

The group watched as the man made his way around the dining room, finally arriving at their table. He addressed Taylor first.

"Deputy Baker?" he asked, and Taylor nodded. Mr. Crenshaw extended his hand. "Oliver Crenshaw. My employees tell me I have you to thank, for quieting down the disturbance out here a few minutes ago. I appreciate your efforts. Thank you."

The men shook hands. Mr. Crenshaw next recognized Lucy, and a smile came to his face. "Ms. Hale, correct? So glad you all could make it."

Lucy introduced the others, and Hannah and Miles said hello. Mr. Crenshaw apologized for the incident. "I hate that your first experience here was tainted by such a ludicrous outburst. I assure you, the marinade recipe is entirely my own."

Miles spoke up. "And a delicious recipe it is, Mr. Crenshaw. We're very much enjoying the food."

"We are," Hannah agreed. "You have a very nice restaurant. I love the atmosphere!"

Oliver Crenshaw smiled. "I'm so glad to hear that. It is my hope that we become a popular spot for family dinners, as well as more intimate gatherings."

"Well, you have our vote," Lucy assured him. "We'll definitely be back."

"Yes, we will. And please call down to the station if you have any more trouble," Taylor instructed the man. "No one has a right to disrupt your patrons like that."

Mr. Crenshaw nodded his thanks. "Hopefully, history will not repeat itself." He turned to Lucy. "I'd love to stop by your bakery. Maybe next week –"

"Help, help! Someone call 911!"

The frantic shout came from the entrance. The group all swiveled their heads to see a man rushing in through the lobby door, his coat half buttoned.

"It's Chef Fugasi! He's collapsed on the sidewalk!"

11

Taylor jumped up, almost knocking over his water glass. "Call 911!" he yelled over his shoulder, bolting for the entrance.

Hurrying after Taylor, Lucy glanced back and saw Hannah had her phone in hand, punching buttons. Miles, standing beside Hannah, motioned for Lucy to go on.

Pushing past the shocked patrons who'd jumped up from their tables, she reached the lobby and saw Dr. Jax was right on Taylor's heels. They flew out the heavy wooden doors together, spilling onto the sidewalk, where a crowd was gathered around the prone chef.

"Back up, people, the doctor is here," Taylor commanded, and the crowd fell back silently, revealing the portly man lying on his back, with his head turned to the side and his mouth partially open.

Dr. Jax crouched next to the big man and felt his neck for a pulse. Lucy held her breath, watching as the doctor's face changed, becoming grim.

"No pulse," he muttered. He hurriedly loosened the chef's collar and began resuscitation attempts.

Lucy watched, one hand clamped over her mouth, the other over her heart, praying, as Dr. Jax applied chest compressions and mouth to mouth, to no avail. The chef lay still and pale, his eyes glassy and unfocused. After five minutes of diligent effort, Dr. Jax sighed and ceased his ministrations.

He looked up at Taylor and shook his head, gently brushing his hand over Fugasi's face, closing the man's eyelids.

"He's gone," Dr. Jax pronounced, his voice subdued.

Seconds later, they could hear the wail of the ambulance echoing down the street.

Lucy felt a presence at her shoulder and looked up, finding Hannah and Miles standing on the steps beside her.

"Is he…?" Hannah whispered, and Lucy nodded, finding herself unable to turn away from the scene. Chef Fugasi, though his body lay unnaturally still, maintained his ruddy complexion, contributing to the illusion he was only sleeping.

"Heart attack?" Miles wondered in a low tone.

Lucy didn't reply, but felt he was probably correct. *Either that or a stroke*, she thought. The chef's renowned temper, combined with his love of rich food—a fact evidenced by the girth of his waistline—made him a prime candidate for coronary disease and hypertension.

The ambulance arrived and Taylor conferred briefly with the paramedics, before turning away and scanning the crowd, locating Lucy on the steps. He hurried over.

"I've got to stick around here for a bit," he announced, his blue eyes apologetic as they connected with Lucy's. He turned to Miles, handing him the keys. "Could you drive the girls' home, please? I'll catch a ride back to the station and pick up my truck later at your house."

"Of course," Miles said, accepting the keys.

Taylor leaned in to kiss Lucy's cheek. "Sorry, honey. We'll have a re-do." She nodded, and he turned away, walking over to a cruiser that was pulling up.

Miles glanced at Hannah. "We'll have a re-do, ourselves," he promised her, and she managed a small smile. Lucy saw the disappointment in her friend's eyes and wished fate had been kinder to Miles and Hannah on their first date.

As the three of them climbed into Taylor's SUV and navigated out of the parking lot, leaving Sizzle Restaurant behind, Lucy looked out the window, reflecting on how different the mood had been just a few short hours ago.

―――

"So, right in the middle of Mr. Crenshaw apologizing for Chef Fugasi's behavior, a man comes rushing in from outside, saying the chef had collapsed on the sidewalk out front." Lucy finished telling the tale and leaned back against the kitchen chair with a sad sigh. Miles and Hannah had declined to come in, and Lucy was filling in her aunt on the tragedy.

Aunt Tricia's eyes were round behind her tortoiseshell glasses. "Oh, my goodness! Do they know what happened?"

Lucy shook her head. "I'm assuming it was natural causes, but of course, we don't know anything yet. Dr. Jax happened to be there eating dinner, and he tried to revive him, but it was too late."

Aunt Tricia looked thoughtful. "It was probably a heart attack. From what I hear, Chef Fugasi was always yelling at someone. He was well known for a bad temper." She shook her head. "Still a sad day, though. Oh, my… his poor wife."

Gigi head-butted Lucy's shin and she reached down, absently scratching the feline's head. "Yes. What a terrible thing. But… on a lighter note, Auntie, Hannah, and Miles got along famously."

Aunt Tricia's eyes took on a gleam of interest. "Did they, now?" Her lips curved.

Lucy nodded. "They have tons of common ground. From absolutely detesting winter to the both of them putting mustard on French fries."

Aunt Tricia wrinkled her nose. "I never understood that habit of Hannah's. Mustard is for hot dogs." She met Lucy's eyes. "And don't they both love animals?"

Lucy nodded emphatically. "I think that's the clincher, there. Hannah's finally found someone who wants to rescue all the homeless pets as much as she does. Miles takes in stray dogs as a temporary stop while they get placed in forever homes."

Aunt Tricia smiled approvingly. "Oh, yes. I can see where that would turn Hannah's head. So, how did they leave it?"

Lucy chuckled. "Well, they've already made plans for another date, and Hannah told me she's planning to invite Miles for dinner next week."

Aunt Tricia looked surprised. "Dinner at her house? But Hannah doesn't cook!"

Lucy looked amused. "Hannah doesn't cook dinner food. But she happens to make excellent pancakes. That's what she's planning on making. Blueberry pancakes." The tragic events of the night faded away, and Lucy's eyes twinkled at the mental image.

Aunt Tricia rolled her eyes. "Well, she better plan on serving both sausage and bacon if she wants to win that man's heart through his stomach. Blueberry pancakes aren't enough to satisfy a man's hearty appetite."

Lucy laughed, letting the tension of the night fall away. "Maybe she'll serve French fries and mustard on the side."

12

Lucy was setting up the cappuccino machine the next morning when Betsy rushed through the bakery door.

"I just found out what happened to Chef Fugasi!" Betsy's eyes were wide. "I can't believe it. Do you think it was foul play?"

Lucy turned away from the machine to look at Betsy curiously.

"Why would you ask that? It looked like a heart attack to me. The man was dead on the sidewalk."

Betsy tucked her purse under the counter and traded her quilted parka for a Sweet Delights Bakery apron, tying the straps around her waist.

"Considering this town's history, it seems a natural question," she pointed out, then looked toward the kitchen, where Hannah was clanging muffin tins. "Forget about that." She lowered her voice to a stage whisper.

"I spoke to Joseph after he talked to Miles. Does Hannah like Miles as much as he likes her?" Her blue eyes sparkled.

Lucy grinned and nodded her head silently, just as Hannah came through the kitchen doorway, bearing a tray of freshly baked muffins.

"Whether or not it was foul play, at least it didn't happen *inside* Sizzle Restaurant," Hannah commented, having heard Betsy's initial question. "Poor Mr. Crenshaw had enough to deal with last night, with the chef disturbing his customers like that."

She set the tray down and began transferring muffins to the pastry case. "Not to speak ill of the dead, but Chef Fugasi was not a nice person, by any account I've heard."

Lucy looked at Hannah, confused. "What do you mean, *whether or not it was foul play*? There wasn't a mark on the chef. He just collapsed."

Hannah met her gaze. "Well, if you think back, was foul play immediately suspected with Paula Peak, when she collapsed at her own author's reading? Or with Jonas Nelson? When you found him dead in the snow at the Christmas tree farm?"

Lucy went quiet, pondering her friend's words. Ivy Creek had seen its share of murders, to be sure. And Hannah was correct, in most cases, the victims had been presumed dead by natural causes, until autopsies were performed.

"Hmm, yes, I see your point. Well, we'll know more soon. I'm sure Taylor will update us on the status of the case as soon as he has a chance." Lucy's brow was furrowed as she completed her task, the seeds of Hannah's words taking root in her mind.

Was this going to turn into another Ivy Creek murder? She sincerely hoped not.

"Well, one good thing is, poor Bert Dobbins is catching a break," Betsy said, stirring a caramel shot into her latte. "He's no longer the prime topic of gossip in town. I stopped for gas at Curtis Wyke's station, on my way in. The scene Chef Fugasi made in the dining room last night at Sizzle, followed by his collapse, is all anyone's talking about."

Hannah was sifting through the day's orders, separating them into piles.

"Wow, Lucy, did you see how many cookie-gram orders have come in? We have..." she re-counted, double checking, then looked up with brows raised.

"Fifty-seven over the next three days."

Lucy grinned. "Well, let's get to work, then!" She tied on her own apron and followed Hannah back into the kitchen.

For the next two hours, Lucy and Hannah rolled out several batches of sugar cookie dough, cutting and baking rectangular-shaped cookie-grams, until both bakery racks were filled with the product waiting to be decorated.

Aunt Tricia came in just before the lunch rush to assist Betsy out front, and with the influx of fresh customers came the addition of fifteen more cookie-gram orders. Betsy appeared in the kitchen doorway to deliver the new orders to Lucy.

Lucy leafed through the sheets, reading the inscriptions, as Hannah lined up the baked cookies on metal tables to be decorated in royal icing.

"Aww... some of these are so sweet," Lucy murmured, her heart touched by the sentiments. She read a few of the inscriptions out loud. "In each other's arms we are complete… You are my moon, sun and stars… How lucky am I to be called yours…"

Betsy nodded, her eyes misting. "It's wonderful to hear all these heartfelt sentiments from the citizens of Ivy Creek. Who knew so much love was out there, in our little town?"

Lucy smiled, thinking the same thing.

Hannah looked over at Betsy. "Are you sending one to Joseph?"

Betsy nodded. "But I haven't figured out what to say yet." She watched as Hannah loaded up pastry bags with colored icing. "My life is so different now that Joseph is in it. I've changed the way I look at things now."

"How so?" asked Lucy, organizing the orders by date needed.

Betsy sighed, her eyes dreamy. "I think about the future all the time. I view things as happening to both of us, not just the impact on me. And I guess I'm more concerned with Joseph's happiness than my own." She paused, adding, "I mean, yes, I want to be happy. But I really, *really* want Joseph to be happy."

"Aww… that just means you're in love…" Lucy smiled at her, and Betsy blushed.

"Yes, I am," she admitted. "But I'm afraid to say that to him. I don't want to rush things."

Aunt Tricia appeared in the doorway behind her. "Oh, pish-posh! That boy is in love with you, too. It's as plain as the nose on your face."

"You think so?" Betsy looked hopeful.

"Yes!" chorused Aunt Tricia, Hannah, and Lucy simultaneously, and Betsy giggled, conceding the point.

"Well… maybe we both are. I hope you guys are right. But I still don't know if a cookie-gram is the best way to tell him. For the first time, anyway."

Hannah countered, "You work in a bakery on Valentine's Day. I think a cookie-gram is the perfect way to tell him."

Betsy smiled but shrugged, not entirely convinced. "We'll see."

"How about Taylor?" asked Aunt Tricia, looking at Lucy. "Are you sending him a cookie-gram?"

Lucy nodded. "I'd better. It wouldn't look good for our deputy sheriff to be dating the bakery owner and not get a Valentine's sweet."

"Hey, what was all that about cats and dogs with you and Taylor at dinner?" asked Hannah. "Did Taylor actually say he was a dog person, not a cat person?"

Lucy tried not to frown. She'd have just as soon forgotten about that. "Well, he didn't say he doesn't like cats, Hannah. Just that he could see himself having dogs."

"And see those dogs sleeping in his bed," Hannah pointed out, and Aunt Tricia's eyebrows shot up.

"In the bed? Oh, no. Gigi would not like that one bit." The older woman shook her head, then eyed Lucy. "Perhaps he was just kidding around."

The phone rang out front, and Betsy hurried out to answer it. Lucy shrugged in answer to Aunt Tricia's comment.

"Maybe. I'm not going to worry about it. It's not like Taylor would ever expect me to give up Gigi." But Taylor's remark prickled Lucy a little bit, as a vision came, unbidden, into her mind: Taylor, herself, Gigi, and two bull mastiffs all crowded onto her queen-sized antique sleigh bed with its rose duvet cover.

"Lucy? It's Taylor on the phone." Betsy reappeared, holding out the receiver.

Lucy tried to banish the image from her mind. "Hi, Taylor. Any news?"

Taylor's voice did the trick, wiping her mental slate clean with the impact of his words.

"Hi, Lucy. I do have news, but not good news. Preliminary results show Chef Fugasi was poisoned."

13

Lucy's mouth dropped open in shock. "Poisoned? From the food at Sizzle?" She saw the shocked looks being exchanged between Betsy and Aunt Tricia.

"At this point we haven't determined that," Taylor clarified. "All I can say is there was zinc phosphide present in the contents of Chef Fugasi's stomach. We're still trying to determine when the poison was introduced into his system."

"Zinc phosphide?" Lucy repeated, her brow furrowed. "Is that a common poison?"

Taylor made an affirmative sound. "It's a rodenticide. Interestingly enough, within the products used for pest control, zinc phosphide smells like garlic."

"Could it have been an accident, then?" Lucy asked hopefully.

Taylor was silent for a heartbeat. "I don't think so," he answered. "I suppose anything's possible, though."

Lucy absorbed his skepticism, her spirit drooping. *In all likelihood, there had been another murder in Ivy Creek.*

She heard voices in the background at Taylor's location and knew she shouldn't keep him. "OK. Thanks for letting us know. Are you doing alright?"

Taylor emitted a dry, humorless chuckle. "Besides second-guessing my career choice, yes. I'm OK, Lucy."

They exchanged goodbyes and Lucy hung up the phone, facing the crew. She repeated what Taylor had found out, and Hannah frowned. "Garlic? Gee whiz, you'd think the manufacturers would lace it with something that smells dangerous, like chemicals, not yummy, like food."

"Well, then the rats wouldn't eat it," Betsy pointed out, logically.

Hannah nodded, adding darkly, "But neither would the chef."

The ladies returned to their tasks, but the news from Taylor hung over the bakery like a dark cloud. As Lucy threw herself into her work, decorating cookie-grams, her mind wandered, no longer finding joy in the sweet messages.

Who would have poisoned Chef Fugasi?

―――――

AUNT TRICIA and Lucy left the closing of the bakery to Hannah and Betsy that afternoon, having discovered they both had errands on the same side of town. Aunt Tricia suggested they combine their trip and pick up a light supper from Rick's Café to take home.

Lucy agreed with mixed feelings, as she and the café owner, Rick, had dated briefly a little more than a year ago, before she and Taylor had decided to give it another try.

While the short-lived romance hadn't ended badly, Lucy had been avoiding Rick's Café since, simply because she felt awkward. The small bistro did offer some delicious fare, however, and she reasoned with herself that it was time to move past her reluctance.

The ladies ordered a Quiche Lorraine and a large Greek salad to take home, dealing with a pleasant young woman whom Lucy had never met. She kept her eyes peeled for Rick to appear, but within a few minutes their transaction was completed, and she and Aunt Tricia left the café without seeing him.

The two strolled down the sidewalk to where they had parked in front of the bookstore.

"Now, that wasn't so bad, was it?" Aunt Tricia commented, and Lucy looked at her sharply.

"What?"

The older woman gave her a knowing look. "Stopping in at Rick's Café. You've been avoiding that place for a year now."

Lucy raised her eyebrows. She hadn't thought her aunt had noticed. "Well, it might have been slightly more awkward if Rick had been there," she pointed out.

Aunt Tricia sighed, shaking her head. "Still time to move on. The two of you are business owners in a very small town. It would do you both good to have each other's backs."

Lucy bristled. "I always had Rick's back! Don't you remember, Auntie? It was Rick who tried to discourage me from expanding the bakery–"

Lucy saw her aunt wasn't listening. Her head was cocked as she focused on something ahead of them on the street. Lucy stopped talking and turned to look, spotting the figure of a man.

It was Oliver Crenshaw, coming out of the five and dime. He had descended the steps, but was standing on the sidewalk, looking back up at the building. He seemed to be arguing with someone, gesturing wildly, and shaking his head.

As Aunt Tricia and Lucy drew nearer, they could hear the belligerent tones of another man before they could even see him.

Lionel Wrigley was slowly descending the steps, pointing his cane at Mr. Crenshaw.

"You should be in jail! Everyone knows it was you who poisoned my chef!"

Mr. Crenshaw's expression was so shocked that Lucy had to wonder if he hadn't been informed of the chef's cause of death yet.

"You're insane!" Crenshaw retorted, backing away from Mr. Wrigley's wavering cane and obvious anger. He looked nervously up and down the street, as if in search of help.

Lucy picked up her pace, feeling bad for the man.

"Mr. Crenshaw. What's going on here?" Lucy reached the man and glared up at Lionel Wrigley, whose face was red with anger. He stood up on the third step, brandishing his cane like a weapon.

"That man…" Mr. Crenshaw sputtered. "What utter nonsense!" He directed his next comment at Mr. Wrigley. "What possible reason would I have to poison your chef? In my own restaurant?" His tone was incredulous.

He looked around beseechingly at the crowd that was beginning to gather.

Lionel Wrigley retorted, "Oh, you had motive, alright! Chef Fugasi had just denounced your marinade recipe in public! A recipe that was stolen from me!" Wrigley looked around at the crowd hoping for support. "My great-great-grandfather's recipe! A family secret, it was. Stolen, by this man!"

"That's ridiculous!" Mr. Crenshaw bristled. "The marinade is a recipe of my own creation! I've spent years developing it, I'll have you know."

"Prove it!" Wrigley countered, and Crenshaw stared at him, uncomprehending.

"What? How?"

Mr. Wrigley leaned on his cane, a speculative expression on his face. "List the ingredients, right here, right now."

Mr. Crenshaw looked horrified. "I'll do no such thing! It's *my* recipe!"

"You stole it from *me*!" Wrigley bellowed loudly, and Lucy pulled out her phone. It was time to get Taylor involved.

Before she could place the call, however, Gill Cameron, who managed the five and dime, appeared in the store's doorway.

"If the two of you don't stop your bickering and go your separate ways right now, I'm calling the police." He glared at the two men, adding, for good measure, "And if I have to do that, you'll both be banned from this store."

Oliver Crenshaw held up both hands in a sign of peaceful acquiescence.

"I'm going," he said, turning on his heel, his back now to Mr. Wrigley. He tipped his hat at Lucy and Aunt Tricia as he walked away. "Ladies…"

Lionel Wrigley stood on the steps, watching him go, a scowl on his face.

"You'll pay for what you've done, Crenshaw," he muttered darkly, then abruptly turned and headed in the opposite direction.

14

"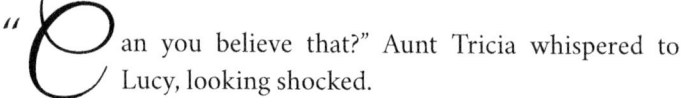an you believe that?" Aunt Tricia whispered to Lucy, looking shocked.

Lucy hesitated, with her phone still in hand. *To call Taylor, or not?*

Aunt Tricia sensed her quandary. "Let's just go home," she suggested. "You can tell Taylor about it later."

Lucy nodded and tucked her phone back into her purse, following Aunt Tricia to their car. As they drove home, she couldn't help but wonder about the future of Sizzle Restaurant. Would this turn of events cause Mr. Crenshaw to close up shop? She hoped not. The more she saw of Lionel Wrigley, the more she became convinced the man was a bully.

They arrived home and settled in for the night, finding the quiche and salad from Rick's Café to be quite delicious. Aunt Tricia had a book club meeting at seven o'clock, so Lucy and Gigi would have the house to themselves.

That evening, Lucy flipped through TV channels listlessly, not finding anything interesting to watch. She paused on a drama showcasing one of her favorite actresses, and tried to let herself be drawn into the plot.

Within a few minutes, it became obvious the heroine of the story was about to have her heart broken. Lucy's hand stilled in the middle of stroking Gigi's silky, white fur as the female character turned an anguished face to the male lead.

"But I thought we had the same vision of a perfect future," the actress whispered. The camera zoomed in for a close-up, showing tears glistening on her lashes as her bottom lip trembled. "Why didn't you tell me you never wanted children?"

Her romantic partner had his back turned to her, but now the camera captured his profile, his handsome face shadowed with regret.

"People change," he said, his voice gruff with emotion. "It was so long ago... we were just kids when we met."

Lucy snapped the TV off, her insecurities about Taylor rising to the surface again.

Did they want the same things from life? Did she even know what she wanted, herself?

"C'mon, Gigi," Lucy murmured. "Let's find a good book to read in bed. Something with a happy ending."

Lucy let herself into the bakery the next morning, wondering how many cookie-gram orders they'd receive today. The way things were going, they'd have to teach Betsy how to hold a pastry bag so she could help write the messages. Although Betsy's penmanship on paper was quite lovely, her few attempts at writing "Happy Birthday" on cakes had been disastrous. She definitely needed practice.

Lucy's phone buzzed with a text message as she flipped on the lights. Setting her bag on the counter, she squinted at the phone. It was Taylor.

Will be searching the restaurant today for evidence. Be in touch.

Lucy tapped out a reply, sighing as she tucked away her phone. Of course, they had to search Sizzle Restaurant, but she knew every day the establishment was closed was only adding to the speculation among the townspeople. She hoped the police would find out what happened quickly, and even better if it all turned out to be an accident.

Aunt Tricia showed up next, yawning, having stayed too late at her book club meeting. Hannah and Betsy arrived almost simultaneously, and after a brief discussion of the best specials to offer for the day, the crew had the bakery up and running, ready to greet their first customers.

"It's a good thing you ordered an extra 50-lb. bag of confectionery sugar," Hannah commented. "We'll have to make another triple batch of royal icing today to keep up with these orders."

"How many cookie-grams do we have left for this week?" Lucy asked, folding pastry boxes and stacking them on a workbench.

Hannah consulted her list. "Thirty-two."

"Make that thirty-three!" Betsy announced, coming into the kitchen. She waved a sheet of paper. "I'm adding my own. Chocolate, please."

Hannah added Betsy's order to the stack, noticing the inscription box was still blank. "Hey, you didn't fill this in. What are we writing?"

Betsy blushed slightly. "Ah… I haven't quite decided, but I will be writing it myself."

Hannah raised her eyebrows and quipped, "Oh? Are you planning to be there to translate the writing for Joseph?"

Lucy snickered and Betsy giggled, not offended. "I've been practicing!"

The phone rang and Lucy picked up the receiver nearest her stacked boxes.

"Sweet Delights Bakery."

"Well, if it isn't my favorite baker," Taylor said in a teasing tone, and Lucy's lips curved into a smile.

"Hi, honey. Are you done over at Sizzle already?"

Taylor replied, "Yes. Nothing suspicious. They did have rat poison with zinc phosphide in the janitorial closet, but there was nothing to indicate it had been used in a criminal manner. Everything in the kitchen was in order. I've cleared the restaurant for re-opening."

"Oh, good! I'm sure Mr. Crenshaw was relieved. Speaking of him…" Lucy relayed what she had witnessed in town the night before.

Taylor sighed. "I'm afraid Lionel Wrigley will continue to be a thorn in Crenshaw's side, despite us finding nothing to implicate Sizzle Restaurant in Chef Fugasi's death."

Lucy privately agreed. Wrigley seemed like a bulldog with a bone. "So, what's next?"

"We're going to retrace the chef's steps, to try and establish where else he went, and what he may have eaten. The answer's got to be in there, somewhere."

"Good luck," Lucy said, wishing she could do something to help. "Let me know what you find out."

They said their goodbyes and Lucy hung up the phone, just as the bell jangled out front.

"Helloooo!" called a familiar voice, and Lucy glanced over at Hannah, who parodied a horrified expression before grinning comically.

The voice belonged to their best customer, Mrs. White, who had a penchant for gossip, and a habit of wiping out entire shelves of pastries to feed her large family.

Lucy heard Aunt Tricia greet Mrs. White, exchanging pleasantries as Lucy rounded the corner.

"I'll take a dozen of the chocolate mint brownies, and six cherry turnovers… oh, hello, Lucy."

"Hi, Mrs. White. How are you today?" Lucy regarded the woman with a smile. Mrs. White was dressed flamboyantly as usual, with a vivid purple faux fur coat, and hot pink earmuffs embellished with red hearts.

"Well, I guess I'm doing better than Lionel Wrigley is now! Why, I'm not sure Wrigley's Steakhouse will be able to go on, without Chef Fugasi. That man was brilliant."

Lucy nodded as Betsy assisted Aunt Tricia in boxing up the woman's pastries. "I guess we'll just have to see what happens," she said noncommittally.

"And I'll take ten of the Valentine's Day cupcakes, too, please," Mrs. White instructed Betsy, before turning back to Lucy.

"Yes, the chef may have been a brilliant man in the kitchen, but oh, my, have I heard stories!" Mrs. White tsked-tsked, looking at Lucy expectantly.

"Stories?" Lucy replied, automatically, but without much interest. She wasn't really in the mood for gossip.

"Why, yes! The man had a temper! I've heard he was given to fits of anger, throwing kitchen utensils, frying pans, and such. And yelling at everyone… Could I also have four of those cinnamon rolls, dear? Thank you."

Mrs. White opened her purse, continuing where she'd left off.

"I've witnessed the man's temper myself! You know, last summer, I was driving home from Red's Corner Market, quite late, maybe at ten o'clock at night? I remember, they were just closing when I left. I happened to glance into Wrigley's Steakhouse parking lot as I drove by, and you'll never guess what I saw!"

Lucy raised her eyebrows. "What did you see?"

Mrs. White's eyes were round as she leaned in closer, lowering her tone.

"That waitress, Mandy something or other. She was standing with Chef Fugasi, and they were arguing something fierce. I could see the expressions on their faces, standing right under the light pole next to a car… her car, I presume - and they both looked furious."

Despite herself, Lucy's interest was piqued. "Oh? I wonder what that was about…"

Mrs. White passed her credit card to Aunt Tricia and shook her head.

"Whatever it was, it looked serious. And... well... intimate." She drew back, looking Lucy in the eye. "Far be it from me to spread rumors, but in my opinion, they were standing entirely too close to each other, for just... co-workers, if you know what I mean." She wiggled her eyebrows, and Lucy frowned.

"Hmm. Well, it was probably nothing. Just an argument, I'm sure. You know what they say, about chefs and tempers." Despite her own words, Lucy tucked that bit of information away, thinking it might be of some importance.

Aunt Tricia handed Mrs. White her card and receipt, and the woman slipped the items into her purse. She gathered up her parcels, stacked one on top of another, and turned to leave the bakery, dispensing some parting words.

"Based on what I saw, I suspect it was more than a work disagreement. The way the chef grabbed Mandy by both arms when she tried to walk away... Well, I'd say it looked like a lovers' quarrel."

15

Lucy's mind was reeling as she watched Mrs. White navigate through the bakery door with her boxes. She wasn't aware of Hannah standing beside her until her friend commented.

"Wow! Do you think it could be true?" Hannah sounded as shocked as Lucy felt. "There was definitely some bad blood between them at the restaurant, but gee whiz… how old was Chef Fugasi, anyway?"

Lucy shook her head, still processing. "I don't know. Late forties? Early fifties?" *And Mandy appeared to be in her mid-twenties,* she thought.

"It wouldn't be the first May-December romance to ever happen," remarked Aunt Tricia dryly. "Not to say it wouldn't be a scandal if it got out. Chef Fugasi was married, you know."

Betsy blinked, obviously stunned as well. "Maybe it's not true. Mrs. White does tend to spread rumors," she reminded them, nibbling her bottom lip.

"But if it is true," Lucy said slowly, "and Mandy served him his food the night he was poisoned..."

The words hung in the air, and Aunt Tricia nudged her. "You need to call Taylor back."

Lucy nodded. Although she'd like to believe it was just a misunderstanding, it was possible that Mrs. White had just handed them a major break in the case. She picked up the phone and walked a few steps away as she dialed Taylor's office.

Taylor answered on the second ring, his voice harried. "Yes? Hello?"

Lucy spoke, hesitation in her voice. "Hi, Taylor, it's me. I just found out something interesting from Mrs. White."

She could hear loud voices in the background, and Taylor called out to someone in an irritated tone. "Yes, it is! I filed it myself!"

He spoke into the receiver, sounding rushed. "Sorry, Lucy. I don't have time right now. I'll have to catch up with you later."

Without another word, he hung up the phone, and Lucy was left staring at the receiver in her hand, a frown on her face. *She knew Taylor was busy, but that was kind of rude.*

She walked back over to the bakery counter and hung up the phone. All three women looked at her expectantly.

"Well? What did he say?" asked Betsy.

Lucy shook her head. "They've got something going on over at the station, and he couldn't talk. I'll tell him later."

She left the three women standing there and went back into the kitchen, unable to get her mind off Mrs. White's story. *Did Mandy have a reason to harm Chef Fugasi?*

Lucy idly flipped through her recipe book, unseeing, instead picturing the unfriendly interaction she'd witnessed between Mandy and the chef at Sizzle.

"Hey, I have an idea."

Lucy looked up, surprised to see Hannah standing there. She'd been so lost in her own thoughts she hadn't noticed her. "What's that?"

Hannah looked speculative. "Mandy lives in the condo building across the street from mine. Why don't we pay her a visit ourselves?"

Lucy tilted her head. "And say what? Ask her if she'd had an affair with Chef Fugasi?"

Hannah nodded. "Exactly. It couldn't hurt. The worst that could happen is she'd tell us to mind our own business. And if she did choose to answer, at least we'd see her face, and could decide if she was telling the truth."

"Hmm…" Lucy ran the scenario through her mind. *Hannah was right. What could it hurt?* "Do you think she's at home?"

Hannah grinned. "Only one way to find out."

———

MANDY ANSWERED the door wearing a lavender-colored robe, with her head wrapped in a damp towel. "Yes?"

Lucy stared at the young woman, tongue-tied, unsure of how to begin.

Hannah smiled. "Hi, Mandy. Can we come in and ask you something?"

Lucy was sure Mandy would refuse, but she surprised her, opening the door and leading the way inside. "I only have a few minutes," she said over her shoulder. "I agreed to work a friend's shift at The Dragon's Lair over in Conover."

Lucy found her voice. "Are you quitting Sizzle, then?"

Mandy shook her head. "No, but we're closed while the police investigate." She settled on the edge of a honey-colored couch and indicated they should sit.

The girls sat down, and Lucy spoke up, glad to have some good news. "Oh, I guess you haven't heard yet. The police cleared Sizzle to reopen."

Mandy lit a cigarette and waved away the smoke. She looked pleased. "That *is* good news. Thanks, you made my night." She took a drag, then looked curiously at the two of them.

"Did you come out here just to tell me that?"

The girls shook their heads in tandem, and Mandy cocked her head.

"What, then?"

Hannah took the lead. "Mandy, I know this is personal, but there's been a report from a reliable source–" she ignored Lucy's raised eyebrows, continuing, "who claims that you and Chef Fugasi were romantically involved last summer. Is it true?"

Lucy froze, inwardly wincing at Hannah's direct approach. Mandy didn't speak for a moment, taking a long drag from her cigarette and blowing out a smoke ring, staring across the room.

She turned to face them, her expression resigned. "Well, I knew it would come out, eventually. Yes, it's true. When I worked at Wrigley's Steakhouse last summer, we had a fling."

She stubbed out her cigarette with more force than necessary. "I must have been insane. The man has serious control issues."

"Had," Hannah interjected, and Mandy nodded.

"Right." She stared out the window. "Well, the affair was a mistake, and I ended it."

Lucy spoke cautiously. "So, you ended it, not the other way around? Because he was married?"

Mandy frowned. "More because he was a jerk, but yeah, I dumped him. And let me tell you, he wasn't too happy about it. He started following me! Every time I turned around, there he was, parked in his car, watching me."

She lit another cigarette. "I quit Wrigley's. I changed my phone number. I stopped going to my old hangouts, but nothing worked. He was like gum stuck to my shoe."

"So, what did you do?" Hannah asked, her voice little more than a whisper.

Lucy knew her friend was wondering if they were about to hear Mandy confess to murder. She was wondering that also and sat gripping the sides of the chair with white knuckles.

Mandy flicked an ash into the ceramic seashell ashtray.

"I did the only thing I could do. I told his wife."

16

"ou told his wife?" Lucy repeated, not sure she'd heard correctly. She glanced at Hannah as Mandy nodded.

"What did his wife say?" Hannah asked, her eyes wide.

Mandy stood up and walked to the window, her cigarette smoke spiraling behind her. She looked back at Lucy and Hannah, lifting a shoulder nonchalantly.

"She said she'd take care of it. And I guess she did, because he stopped bothering me."

She turned, stooping to tap her ash before adding, "I need to go get ready for work."

Speechless, Lucy and Hannah followed Mandy to the front door, thanking her for her time. The door shut softly behind them, and the pair looked at each other, dumbfounded.

"Well, that was certainly odd," commented Lucy as they walked away.

A JUICY STEAK TRAGEDY

Hannah shook her head skeptically. "I'm not buying it. Something's off with that story."

Lucy was silent, trying to picture the scenario. She really needed to get Taylor's take on this. She and Hannah parted ways, as Hannah lived just across the street, and Lucy got back into her car, trying to come up with a plan to validate the information.

THE OPPORTUNITY PRESENTED itself that evening, in the form of an apologetic text from Taylor.

So sorry I was short on the phone earlier. Want company?

Lucy thought for a minute, then tapped out a reply.

Too tired. Got an errand in the morning. Come with me? Won't take long.

She waited, still hatching her plan, when Taylor's response came through.

Absolutely. Where are we going?

Lucy smiled, sending out her reply.

A sympathy visit to Mrs. Fugasi

Lucy nestled the casserole dish and tray of pastries in the backseat of Taylor's SUV and got into the passenger seat, buckling up.

Taylor looked at her. "Ready?"

Lucy nodded, and they set off. They rode in silence for a few minutes, and then Lucy flashed him a smile. "I'm glad you're coming with me."

He smiled back. "Happy to. It's awfully sweet of you to pay her a visit. I'm sure she'll appreciate the food."

Lucy nodded, slightly uncomfortable. She needed to tell Taylor what was going on.

"So… Hannah and I happened to run into Mandy Taft, the waitress at Sizzle…" Without further ado, Lucy launched into the story of the chef's affair, hoping Taylor wouldn't scold her for being too nosy.

They stopped at a red light, and Taylor turned to look at her. His face showed his shock. "I can't believe that! Do you think Mandy was telling the truth?"

Lucy shrugged. "I don't know why she would lie." She left it at that, knowing Taylor would take the bull by the horns and question Mrs. Fugasi himself. Her role in this visit was now purely one of a sympathetic member of the community.

They pulled into the driveway of the Fugasi residence, and were greeted by a small white dog, barking insistently, who sat on the front porch. Mrs. Fugasi appeared at the door, scooping up the animal and ushering them inside.

"Oh, my, thank you so much," the woman said, upon seeing the casserole and platter of sweets. "I do appreciate your kindness. Just set them in the kitchen, right there."

Lucy set the tray down and looked around, admiring the large kitchen with stainless steel appliances. The room was spotless and bright, aided by a skylight over the kitchen island countertop.

"Some coffee or tea?" Mrs. Fugasi offered, and Taylor accepted a coffee. Lucy politely declined.

They took a seat in the living room while Mrs. Fugasi fussed in the kitchen, and they could hear her talking to her little dog. She came out within minutes, setting Taylor's steaming mug on the glass tabletop, and taking a seat across from them.

Lucy addressed the woman with sincerity. "I am so sorry about your husband. If there's anything I can do…"

Mrs. Fugasi compressed her lips, shaking her head. Her face was lined with sorrow.

Although her hair was neatly brushed, she wore a dressing gown, and her face was devoid of makeup. Lucy noticed the woman had left the drapes shut in the living room, a somber contrast to the brightness of the kitchen.

"Thank you," she told Lucy, then addressed Taylor. "Have you found out how it happened?"

Taylor shook his head. "We're still investigating, but at this time, there's no conclusive evidence of tainted food at Sizzle. It may have happened elsewhere or even have been an accident. We simply don't know yet."

He shifted position, slipping into his investigative persona. "Mrs. Fugasi, it's come to my attention during the course of this investigation that your husband may have…" He hesitated, choosing his words carefully. "Been involved with someone."

Mrs. Fugasi sighed. "Yes, yes. I do hope this doesn't find its way into the papers."

Lucy was surprised. "So, you knew about the affair?"

Mrs. Fugasi scoffed. "Affair, as in one?" She shook her head in disgust. "My husband had a very hard time being faithful. Let's leave it at that."

Taylor frowned. "I'm afraid I can't just leave it at that. Was Mandy Taft his most recent indiscretion?"

Mrs. Fugasi nodded, her face weary. "Yes. As far as I know."

Taylor drummed his fingers on his knee. "And when did that affair end?"

Mrs. Fugasi pursed her lips, thinking back. "Before the holidays. Sometime last fall. The girl actually came to me, which I find a bold move. Honestly, at first, I thought it was a shakedown." She shook her head. "She told me she was sorry to have gotten involved with him. I sent her on her way, and never heard another word."

Taylor was silent for a moment. "Did you and your husband fight about his infidelity?"

Mrs. Fugasi regarded Taylor with a wry expression. "I learned early on in my marriage that it did no good to complain. I just ignored his dalliances and prayed it would stay out of the papers."

Lucy marveled silently at Mrs. Fugasi's attitude. *Did she love her husband so much, then, that she'd stay married to him at any cost? Or did she just not care?*

Taylor sipped his coffee thoughtfully, and Mrs. Fugasi posed a question of her own.

"This poison you found in my husband's system. Could it have been administered earlier in the day? Hours before he collapsed?"

Taylor set his cup down. "It's hard to pinpoint exactly when. According to the coroner, there was quite a lot of undigested content in the chef's stomach–" he glanced at Lucy and Mrs. Fugasi apologetically. "Not to be indelicate."

Mrs. Fugasi pressed. "So, the poison may have been in what he ate for lunch that day while he was working?"

Taylor frowned and leaned forward. "Why do you ask? Do you have information about something he'd eaten earlier?"

Mrs. Fugasi reflected silently for a moment, then looked at Taylor and Lucy.

"Adam was no longer happy working for Lionel Wrigley," she informed him. "And he'd just given his notice. He told me Lionel became quite upset with him, claiming if Adam left, it would be a death knell for Wrigley's Steakhouse."

Lucy was confused. "I'm sorry, I don't follow you." She glanced at Taylor, seeing he was puzzled as well.

"My husband was planning to open his own restaurant," Mrs. Fugasi announced, shocking them even further with her next words.

"I think Lionel Wrigley may have poisoned him."

17

Lucy's head was still spinning as she and Taylor climbed back into his vehicle a few minutes later. Mrs. Fugasi's suspicions about Lionel Wrigley had come as a complete surprise, and now Lucy was trying to make sense of it all.

"So… what do you think?" she asked Taylor as he backed out of the driveway. "Is Lionel Wrigley now a suspect?"

"Everyone's a suspect," Taylor replied tersely. "But I have to admit, I wasn't expecting that."

"How about Mrs. Fugasi?" Lucy asked. "Do you believe she was content to just stand by and watch as her husband ran around town with other women?"

Taylor blew out a breath, drumming his fingers on the steering wheel at a stoplight. "I can't pretend to understand it, but it seems as though Mrs. Fugasi had long ago resigned herself to her husband's affairs. So, the question is, if she did poison him, why now? What's changed?"

Lucy pondered the question. "Money? Maybe she took out an insurance policy?"

Taylor nodded, pulling into the bakery to drop Lucy off. "I plan to look into their finances next. We'll see if she had anything to gain. If not, I guess we're back to square one."

"Except for Lionel Wrigley," Lucy reminded him. "We have to consider him as a suspect, now that we know the chef was quitting his job at Wrigley's."

Taylor sighed. "If that's even true. I need to find someone who can corroborate that information."

Lucy leaned over and kissed his cheek. "Thanks for going with me."

"Anytime. Do you need a ride home tonight?"

Lucy shook her head. "I'll get a ride with Aunt Tricia." She exited the vehicle and waved before turning toward the bakery.

As she opened the bakery door, letting the enticing scent of apple-cinnamon bread waft out, she couldn't help but think about the life that Mrs. Fugasi had endured, caught in an unhappy marriage.

Had the chef's wife been driven to murder?

———

"I'm not buying it," Hannah said, shaking her head. She and Lucy were turning loaves of apple-cinnamon bread out of their pans. "Mandy's story sounds fishy to me."

Lucy was surprised. "What part?"

Hannah set dirty loaf pans in the double sink. "That she broke it off with him. Yes, you have Mrs. Fugasi's corroboration that Mandy came to her, but the woman never said Mandy asked her to intervene, correct?"

Lucy shook her head, nibbling on a stray morsel of cinnamon streusel. "She just said that Mandy apologized for getting involved with him."

Hannah turned on the tap, running water for the pans to soak. "Exactly. Which sounds to me like a heads-up, hey-I'm-sleeping-with-your-husband type of visit. Mandy probably thought Mrs. Fugasi would divorce him if she found out."

Lucy wasn't convinced. "Are you saying you think Mandy wanted to marry Chef Fugasi?"

Hannah wiped her hands on a towel, returning to clean the workbench. "I'm just saying I don't think we have the whole story."

Lucy was silent for a moment. "I'm not sure who we could ask, though. Who even knew Mandy and the chef were involved?"

Hannah turned to her with a grin. "Her co-workers at Wrigley's probably knew. You can't keep something like that secret in a kitchen."

Lucy raised her brows. *Hannah had a point.* "What do you say about us stopping in over there for lunch?"

Hannah smiled. "If you're buying, count me in."

THE DINING ROOM of Wrigley's Steakhouse was mostly empty when Lucy and Hannah arrived just after one o'clock. The hostess led them to a table by the window, offering menus and telling them their waitress would be with them shortly.

Lucy looked around, sipping at her water. She hadn't been in here since before her parents had died, but growing up, Wrigley's had been the go-to spot for celebration dinners. It looked much the same.

Hannah decided on a cheeseburger, and Lucy a tuna melt. They set their menus down, and a waitress appeared almost immediately. Lucy read her name tag: *Marcia.*

"Hello, ladies. Have you decided?"

The girls placed their orders, and Lucy hid her smile as Hannah requested mustard to go with her French fries. Jotting their orders down on a pad, Marcia assured them their food would be out in a jiffy.

Hannah looked toward the kitchen's double doors. "Gee, I wonder who they have as a chef now?"

Lucy speculated. "I bet they're scrambling to find someone good. Right now, I suspect one of the assistants is having to step up to the plate." She wondered if Lionel Wrigley had already put the word out before Chef Fugasi had died, knowing the man was quitting.

Marcia brought their food out in short order, setting a mustard dispenser next to Hannah's plate. "Can I get anything else for you, ladies?"

Lucy glanced at Hannah, and her friend took the lead, looking around the dining room. "Last time I was here - I believe it was last summer - there was a waitress named Mandy working. Do you know her?"

Marcia frowned slightly. "Mandy doesn't work here anymore. Are you two friends?"

Hannah shook her head. "No. Just wondering. She just stuck in my memory, is all. Maybe because it was an exceptional meal."

Marcia compressed her lips. "I'm surprised she got your order right. Mandy was always mixing up tables. We got a lot of complaints during her shifts."

Hannah leaned forward, lowering her tone conspiratorially. "I heard a rumor, and I've been wondering ever since. About Mandy and the chef…" She let that dangle, watching Marcia for a reaction. The waitress did not disappoint her.

Glancing around the room first, Marcia then spoke quietly. "They were involved. I think that's the only reason Mandy lasted here as long as she did."

Marcia's face took on a somber expression as she continued. "I don't know if you guys have heard, but Chef Fugasi died a few days ago, of unknown causes." She looked around again to see if she was being overheard. "We're not supposed to tell customers that, that he's gone, I mean."

"Yes, we had heard that. Have they found a replacement yet?" Lucy asked, stirring her ice water with a straw.

Marcia shook her head. "Mr. Wrigley is in the kitchen right now because he doesn't trust anyone else with the marinade recipe. I suppose he'll have to find someone soon, though."

She turned to leave, and Lucy hastened to pose one more question. "Marcia, did you ever hear any rumors about Chef Fugasi intending to open his own restaurant? Had he given notice to Mr. Wrigley?"

Marcia looked surprised at the question. "Gosh, no. Chef Fugasi had worked for Mr. Wrigley forever." She regarded Lucy curiously. "Why would you ask that?"

Lucy hesitated, not knowing what to say, and Hannah came to her rescue.

"It must have been awkward for him here, even after Mandy had quit. If everyone in the kitchen knew she'd dumped him…"

Marcia blanched slightly, frowning and shaking her head.

"Mandy didn't dump him. Chef Fugasi ended their affair. And Mandy took the break-up very badly."

18

Hannah gave Lucy a knowing look before turning to Marcia. "Oh, I see."

Marcia suddenly looked uncomfortable. "Can I get you anything else?"

Hannah and Lucy shook their heads. Marcia smiled politely at them and walked away.

"I told you…" Hannah said softly in a sing-song voice. "Mandy lied."

"Apparently so," murmured Lucy. "I'll call Taylor tonight and see what he thinks."

The girls quietly ate their lunches, paid their bill, and were back at the bakery within the hour.

They entered through the back and walked into the kitchen space, surprised to find Betsy filling a pastry bag with royal icing.

"Gone for an hour, and now she's doing our job for us," joked Hannah, and Betsy blushed.

The younger girl held the vinyl pastry bag with one messy hand, wielding a spatula with the other. Icing was smeared all over her hand and wrist, and Lucy took pity on her.

"Here, let me fix that for you," she offered, taking the sticky bag from Betsy and wiping it with a cloth. Pulling it straight, she demonstrated.

"To avoid a mess, first you fold over the top of the bag, making a cuff. Now when you scoop the icing in, it won't get all over the outside. Like this… see?"

Betsy nodded with a grateful smile and accepted the bag from Lucy. She filled it with icing and twisted the top.

"Now if I could only think of what to write on Joseph's cookie-gram," she said, her brow furrowed. The freshly baked cookie lay on the table in front of her.

"Whatever you decide, I recommend practicing on the bench first," Lucy warned. "It will be difficult to scrape it off the cookie if you make a mistake."

"Don't make her nervous!" Hannah chided with a wink.

"Oh, I'm more nervous about the message itself than I am the writing of it," Betsy assured her. "I mean, it's Valentine's Day, and I love him. I'd like to say that but I'm… I just…" she trailed off, biting her lip.

"Take the leap," Lucy advised. "You know he loves you, too."

"Then why hasn't he said so?" Betsy countered, making experimental squiggles of icing on the metal workbench.

"Because he's a man," Aunt Tricia replied from the archway to the front. They all turned to look. "Men don't think of things like that until women make them think of it."

Betsy asked timidly, "Do you need me to help out front, Tricia? I only meant to be gone a minute."

Aunt Tricia waved her hand. "Take your time, Betsy. Things are pretty slow this afternoon."

Just as she finished speaking, the bell jangled on the front door, and Aunt Tricia peeked around the corner. She looked over at Hannah, a satisfied smile on her face.

"Well, you got back just in time," she said. "I believe this customer would rather deal with you."

Hannah's face lit up with a grin. "Is it Miles?" she asked in a stage whisper, and Aunt Tricia nodded. Hannah looked at Lucy next, mild panic on her face.

"Do I look OK?" she asked, smoothing a hand over her hair. Lucy nodded, and Hannah took a breath, closing her eyes briefly before going out front. Lucy trailed behind her.

"Hello, Miles," Hannah greeted the tall, red-haired man. Her words were echoed by Aunt Tricia and Lucy.

"Hannah," Miles said, his eyes running over her face as if starved for the sight of her. He nodded at Lucy and Tricia. "Hello, ladies."

Betsy's voice was heard calling from the kitchen. "Hello to Miles!"

He chuckled. "Hello to Betsy," he called. He quirked an eyebrow at Lucy. "Have you got Betsy baking, now?"

Lucy grinned. "She's working on a special project."

Hannah smiled at Miles. "What brings you here today? In search of sweets?"

Miles shook his head. "Just you."

Hannah's smile got wider. "Well, here I am."

Miles grinned back at her. "I wanted to solidify our plans for a do-over date. I know we had tentatively said either Wednesday or Thursday. Joseph needs me at the theater Wednesday night, though."

Hannah cocked her head. "I thought the show only ran on the weekends?"

Miles nodded. "I'm afraid we're having to re-cast Romeo. Bert Dobbins said he'll do one more performance, but then he's stepping down. Joseph wants to have a casting call on Wednesday."

"Bert's stepping down?" Lucy asked, disappointed by the news. "Oh, no. Is it because…?"

Miles finished her sentence. "He's too embarrassed after what happened on opening night with Daphne. I have to give him credit, though. He gave it a good try, coming back from that, but, well," he shrugged his shoulders. "I can't say I blame him."

The ladies all murmured their agreement.

"Poor Bert," said Aunt Tricia with a sigh. "Oh, well. I'm sure the right girl will come along for him."

Miles looked into Hannah's eyes, holding her gaze intently. "So, Thursday, then?"

Hannah seemed mesmerized, unable to look away. She nodded. "Dinner at my place."

Miles nodded and smiled. He turned away, heading for the door. Waving goodbye to Hannah, Lucy and Tricia, he called out, with one hand on the doorknob. "Goodbye to Betsy!"

A faint voice floated out of the kitchen. "Goodbye to Miles!"

The bell jangled as he left. Lucy turned to look at Hannah, finding her friend staring dreamily through the bakery window, watching Miles walk away. Lucy chuckled and left her to it, walking back through the kitchen archway.

"How's it going?"

Betsy was leaning over the worktable, intently focused, as she piped icing onto the cookie-gram. Lucy watched, noting that Betsy held the bag exactly as she should, one hand guiding the tip, the other gripping it near the top to control the flow of icing. She was impressed. Betsy had indeed been practicing.

Betsy finished her task and sighed, setting the bag down. She studied her work critically.

"I think I can live with that," she said.

"May I see?" asked Lucy, and Betsy nodded.

Lucy walked to the table and looked down at Joseph's cookie-gram. The stark contrast of white icing on chocolate was pleasing to the eye, and Betsy had done a surprisingly good job with the loops and swirls bordering the rectangle. In the center of the cookie-gram she'd drawn a smiling sun with heart-shaped eyes, and her writing was centered above and below.

With you in my life, there are no cloudy days

"What do you think?" Betsy asked nervously. "Too hokey? I decided to go with light and fun, instead of intensely romantic."

Lucy grinned as she looked into Betsy's worried blue eyes.

"I think it's absolutely perfect."

19

Stifling a yawn, Lucy shuffled into the kitchen in her robe and slippers. The smell of fresh-brewed coffee welcomed her. She needed that jolt of caffeine. Yesterday's revelations regarding Mandy Taft had kept her tossing and turning all night—especially since she was unable to reach Taylor to share what she'd learned. She'd left two voicemails for him, but he'd not returned her call, so she'd finally gone to bed just after midnight. Her sleep had been far from restful.

Blinking in the bright and sunny kitchen, she saw Aunt Tricia standing near the window, looking out at the backyard. Gigi sat at her feet, swishing her tail with her ears slightly flattened. Whatever had caught Aunt Tricia's attention was also being observed by Gigi, and the feline did not look pleased.

"Good morning," Lucy said, reaching for a mug and pouring herself a cup of coffee. She walked over to join the pair at the window. "What are we looking at?"

Aunt Tricia pointed to the juniper trees at the edge of the yard. "There. Do you see him?"

Lucy stepped closer to the window and squinted, at first not knowing what she was looking for. Then a gray and white tabby cat poked his face out, staring back at her.

"Oh! A kitty. I've never seen that one before."

Aunt Tricia turned to her. "Neither have I, but I wish he'd go back home. He was sniffing at the cat door a few minutes ago and got Gigi all riled up. She was about to go out and do her business when she spotted him. Now she won't go out. I tried to scare him away, but that's as far as he went."

Lucy glanced down at her own cat, who was keeping her eyes trained on the intruder. "She hasn't been outside?" Gigi always visited the back yard first thing in the morning, before Lucy and Aunt Tricia left for work.

Aunt Tricia shook her head. "It's a good thing we still keep a litter box for her in the laundry room. I don't think she's going to go out while that cat is still hanging around."

Lucy watched as the gray kitty warily emerged from the bushes, sniffing at the ground. He followed his nose, nimble steps leading him to the edge of the patio.

Gigi growled as he came closer, and Lucy shushed her. "He's not going to hurt you, Gigi." She turned to Aunt Tricia. "Do you think he's a stray?"

"Hard to say. He doesn't look terribly skinny, but then again, he's not wearing a collar. He could just be a good hunter."

"He might have slipped his collar," Lucy said. "I sure hope some small child isn't crying her eyes out because she lost her kitty." She set her cup on the counter. "I'm going to see if I can make friends with him."

As she began to open the door, Gigi skedaddled, running pell-mell for the safety of the hallway. Lucy shook her head. "Silly girl."

She stepped out onto the patio and the gray cat froze, six feet away. Lucy crouched down and extended her hand.

"It's OK, I want to be friends." She made a few kissing sounds, but the cat spooked, taking off for the row of junipers. He peered warily at Lucy from the cover of the low branches, clearly not wanting to be friends.

Lucy straightened up. "OK, have it your way." She slipped back inside the kitchen.

She and Aunt Tricia chatted over a light breakfast, and a short time later, Lucy looked at the clock. It was time to get ready for work. As she walked back toward her bedroom, she could hear Gigi in the laundry room, scratching litter in her box.

It appeared Gigi was planning to stay inside.

LUCY RESTED her hands on the wheel, staring at the detour sign ahead. Usually, her route to work took less than twenty minutes, but the repaving of Columbus Avenue had begun, and now she'd have to loop around the other side of town.

She grumbled to herself as she took the detour, trying to think of a shortcut, but came up blank. Resigned, she traveled the less than familiar road, wondering if she should use her GPS.

Glancing up, she saw a sign for Hearts and Paws at the end of a long driveway. The name rang a bell, and she searched her memory, finally realizing this was the animal shelter that Daphne Bell managed. On impulse, Lucy turned down the driveway. Maybe Daphne would know if someone was missing a gray tabby cat.

There were two cars in the shelter's lot, and Lucy hoped that meant the shelter was open. It was just shy of nine o'clock.

She exited her car and walked up the flagstone path, seeing kennels at the back of the property. The door was unlocked, so Lucy let herself in.

There was no one at the front desk. "Hello?" Lucy called out, but no one answered. She hesitated, not sure if she should sit and wait or go looking for Daphne. She decided to sit for a minute, anyway.

She had just taken a seat when she heard another door open and shut at the back of the building, and the low murmur of voices could be heard. Rising, Lucy walked to the beginning of the corridor and peered down its length. There was no one in sight, but she could hear two people in quiet conversation, so she walked in that direction.

One of the examining rooms had the door open, with bright light spilling into the hallway. Reaching the room, Lucy peered around the doorframe, intending to call Daphne's name. She froze, the words dying on her lips, as she took in the scene in front of her.

Dr. Jax stood with his back to Lucy and his arms wrapped around Daphne in a warm embrace. Daphne's eyes were closed in contentment as she rested her chin on his shoulder, unaware of Lucy standing a few feet away.

All at once, Daphne's eyes flew open, and she spotted Lucy.

"Oh!"

20

Lucy stammered, her face going red as she backed up a step. "I… I'm sorry!" She turned and walked quickly back to the waiting room, her mind whirling.

Daphne and Dr. Jax?

Behind her, she heard Daphne call out. "I'll be right there, Lucy!"

There were muffled voices and then two pairs of footsteps sounded in the hallway. Dr. Jax appeared first, headed for the front door.

Lucy glanced up, catching his eye and mouthing, "Sorry." The doctor's face remained pleasant, but he didn't stop to talk, merely nodding politely to her before exiting the building. Lucy cringed. Clearly, he was as embarrassed as she.

Daphne appeared next, smoothing her hands over her hair. Her face was composed and held a trace of humor. "Well, you've found us out," she quipped in a light tone.

Lucy shook her head contritely. "I'm so sorry to have intruded like that. I don't know what I was thinking—I should have just stayed here in the lobby."

Daphne waved away her apology. "It's no big deal, Lucy. We've been keeping our dating a secret, but mostly for Bert's sake. He's been through enough."

"So, Bert doesn't know?" Lucy asked. In such a small town, it was extremely hard to keep any secrets.

Daphne shook her head. "I don't think so. It's ironic, really. Bert once accused me of being attracted to Keith—Dr. Jax, I mean—while he and I were still a couple, but it was just because we spend so much time in each other's company, caring for the animals here. Then, after Bert and I broke up, Keith asked me out to coffee, and… well, it was just meant to be, I guess. Everything clicked."

Lucy assured her. "Your secret's safe with me, Daphne."

Daphne smiled. "Thanks. So, what brings you here this morning? Looking to adopt?"

Lucy chuckled. "No, my cat's not ready for a companion - which is actually why I'm here. Has anyone reported a gray and white tabby cat missing? There's suddenly one hanging around in my yard."

Daphne shook her head. "I haven't heard of any reports, but I'll make a few calls. Is it a boy or a girl?"

Lucy shrugged. "I don't know, really, but I have a feeling it's a boy. He's got my kitty, Gigi, quite upset."

Daphne chuckled. "Ah, she probably sees him as a rival for food. I'll put the word out."

"Thanks, Daphne." Lucy looked at her watch. "I've got to get to the bakery."

The ladies parted ways, and Lucy got into her car, reflecting on Daphne and Dr. Jax as a romantic couple while she drove through town. Now that she'd gotten over her initial shock, she could see the two of them were likely very compatible, since the welfare of animals was their mutual focus.

Poor Bert. He's not going to be happy when he finds out.

Lucy was sitting upstairs in her office just after lunch when her cell phone rang. She glanced at the display. *Taylor.* She picked up the receiver.

"You're a hard man to track down," she said by way of greeting.

"I'm sorry, Lucy," Taylor's voice was apologetic. "I've been running down a lead and I think we're finally getting somewhere."

"Oh?" Lucy sat up straighter. "Care to share? I found out some things, too."

"Why am I not surprised you've been investigating on your own?" Taylor replied in a wry tone. "You go first."

Lucy sat back, leaning her head against the headrest. "First off, I think Mandy Taft was lying about being the one to break up with Chef Fugasi."

She quickly filled in Taylor on the visit to Wrigley's Steakhouse with Hannah. "So, I'm thinking maybe the chef was going to end their affair and Mandy went to Mrs. Fugasi, thinking she'd divorce her husband if she found out. But then it backfired - that could be the argument Mrs. White witnessed in the parking lot." She paused for a moment. "And then Mandy saw an opportunity for revenge when the chef came into Sizzle Restaurant."

Taylor went silent, pondering her words. He finally replied, "That is entirely possible, but so far, we have nothing else that backs up your theory. No source of the poison. No witnesses."

Lucy sighed. He was right. "OK, so what did you find out?"

"Mrs. Fugasi took out a very large life insurance policy on her husband just fifteen months ago. Once it's been settled, she'll become a very rich woman."

Lucy absorbed that information. *Mrs. Fugasi had a motive, alright. And opportunity to slip a pesticide into her husband's food.*

"Are you any closer to finding out a timeline on the poison?" she asked. "Or narrowing it down to a certain food he'd eaten? The only thing he'd eaten at Sizzle was a juicy steak."

Taylor replied, "Not yet, but we have our best in forensics working on it." Lucy heard a muffled sound and realized it was Taylor yawning.

"You should pop in over here for a quick pick-me-up," she suggested. "A little caffeine and some sugar would do you some good."

Truth be told, she missed Taylor. That darned compatibility quiz was still bouncing around in the back of her mind, and she needed some good, old-fashioned, one-on-one time with her beau to banish her insecurities.

"Can't," he replied regretfully. "I just got a call from Dr. Jax about his garage being vandalized. I need to stop over there and talk to him."

"You're kidding," Lucy said, thinking of Dr. Jax and Daphne. *Should she tell Taylor what she'd found out?* "What happened?"

Taylor sighed. "Someone smashed all the windows and broke in. You know that fancy sports car he only brings out once or twice a year? Apparently, the vandals smashed that up, too."

Lucy frowned. "Vandals? So, you think it was more than one person?"

Taylor made an affirmative sound. "Oh, I have my suspicions about who it was. Last week I personally caught Jack Lomax, Hayden Koontz, and Stevie Allman smashing mailboxes down on Highland Creek Road. Sounds like one of their pranks to me."

Lucy was surprised. The boys he'd mentioned were just teenagers. "Why would they target Dr. Jax? Everyone loves him."

"Bored? On a dare? I don't know, but I'm guessing it's their handiwork. I'll go have a talk with their parents, see where they were last night. I'd be willing to bet it was those kids prowling around Dr. Jax's house the other night, too, setting off the alarm."

"Didn't Dr. Jax say there was only one prowler?"

Taylor corrected her. "He only *saw* one prowler. But it was probably that bunch, up to no good."

Lucy looked at the clock, thinking she needed to get back to work. "Hmm. Good luck with that. So, are you planning to have a talk with Mandy yourself? Or with her co-workers?"

Taylor sounded noncommittal. "I need to see where this lead with the chef's wife goes first. Money is the motive in over ninety percent of all murder cases, you know."

They said their goodbyes, and Lucy hung up the phone, sitting back and reflecting on what Taylor had said. She couldn't really see Mrs. Fugasi taking her husband's infidelity in stride for so many years, and then suddenly poisoning him. Something didn't add up.

Money might be the number one reason for murder, but unrequited love was probably a close second. From what the waitress Marcia had said, Mandy was a woman scorned.

21

The brisk February morning air preceded her as Betsy sailed through the bakery's front door, calling out, "Good morning!"

Her voice was cheerful and bright, and she looked as though she were walking on air.

Lucy grinned. "So, I'm guessing your cookie-gram went over well?" Although she'd decorated it days before, Betsy had only presented it to Joseph last night.

Betsy smiled radiantly. "He loved it!"

"He loves *you*," Aunt Tricia corrected her, with a smile in her voice. "It wouldn't matter if you'd scribbled on a saltine cracker with a magic marker. That man would have told you it was the best thing he'd ever eaten."

Betsy giggled, amused by the image. "Well, I imagine my cookie-gram was a bit more yummy than an ink-infused saltine, but thank you for saying so." She tucked her belongings away and reached for her apron. "Where's Hannah?"

Lucy finished counting out bills and tucked them into the register. "I gave her today off. Last night was her big, at-home dinner date with Miles."

Betsy pouted. "But I want to know how it went!"

Lucy chuckled. "I guess you could call her and ask her, if you can't wait until tomorrow."

Betsy harrumphed. "I'll wait." She looked at Lucy speculatively. "Does that mean you need me working in the kitchen with you today? I can help you decorate cookie-grams."

Lucy looked at Aunt Tricia first. "If you don't need Betsy out here, I could use her help."

"Go on then," Aunt Tricia smiled indulgently at Betsy. "If we get a morning rush, I'll give you a shout."

Happily, Betsy poured herself a coffee and followed Lucy into the kitchen. Lucy set her up with a stack of orders and a pastry bag full of icing.

"The cookies are all on that rack, chocolate and vanilla. Take your time," she advised. "Practice piping a little on the bench first."

Betsy nodded and Lucy set up her own station, lining up cookie-grams to be decorated.

"How did try-outs go the other day? Did Joseph find a new Romeo?"

Betsy nodded, her eyes on her work as she carefully outlined a cookie-gram with icing. "Yes, he might not be as good as

Bert, but he did a pretty good reading. His name is Justin King, and he's a sophomore at the college."

"Oh, good!" Lucy said. "So, the show goes on. I'm going to try to get Taylor to bring me, but he's a hard sell on theater. It might be that I wind up going with Aunt Tricia instead."

"Romeo and Juliet should be seen with your boyfriend, not your aunt," Betsy murmured. She glanced up with a mischievous look. "You can tell Taylor I said so."

Lucy smiled. "I might just do that."

A short time later, the front bell rang, and voices could be heard as Aunt Tricia greeted a customer. She poked her head through the archway.

"Lucy, Oliver Crenshaw is here wanting to talk to you."

Lucy looked up, surprised. She set her bag down and wiped her hands on a rag. "OK, let me wash up, and I'll be right there."

A minute later, Lucy rounded the corner, seeing the restaurateur waiting patiently, his hands clasped behind his back while he looked out the window.

"Mr. Crenshaw," Lucy greeted him. "What can I do for you?"

He turned around with a smile. "Please, call me Oliver. It's nice to see you again, Ms. Hale."

"Lucy, please," she said, and he nodded, tucking his thumbs into his belt loops.

"Lucy it is. Do you have a minute to talk?"

Lucy nodded, gesturing to a table. He took a seat.

"Can I get you anything?" she asked. "A coffee?"

"No, thank you," he said, and Lucy slid into the chair across from him.

Oliver cleared his throat. "As you probably know, Sizzle Restaurant has re-opened."

Lucy nodded. "Yes, I've heard. How's business?"

Oliver compressed his lips. "Very poor, I'm afraid. I believe the tragic death of Chef Fugasi may have done irreparable damage to my chances in this town. It's been several days since we've re-opened, but we're hardly getting any traffic at all."

Lucy frowned. "Oh, no. I'm so sorry to hear that!"

Oliver looked glum. "Yes, well, I can hardly blame people for being reluctant to eat in a restaurant where someone recently died—of poison, no less. I was hoping that the public statement Deputy Baker made, clearing Sizzle of any wrong doing, would be enough to restore the townsfolk's faith in my restaurant, but apparently not." He met Lucy's eyes. "That's why I'm here. I think you may be able to help."

Lucy was puzzled. "Me? How so?"

Oliver gestured at the bakery front. "Not you, so much as Sweet Delights Bakery. Since you're such an established business here in town, I thought maybe if Sizzle started to carry some sweets and breads from your bakery, then people might begin to trust us again."

He studied her face. "Of course, I'm not trying to pressure you in any way. If you'd rather not be involved with Sizzle-"

Lucy interrupted him. "No, I'd be happy to help."

His countenance brightened. "You would? That's great! Thanks, Lucy."

Lucy smiled. "You're welcome. I'll send a wholesale price list your way this afternoon."

"Very good." Oliver fished a business card from his shirt pocket. "My email address is on the back." He glanced at his watch.

"I should be going. I'm interviewing several candidates for a waitress position."

Lucy cocked her head, surprised, as he'd just told her business was slow. Oliver caught her puzzled expression and elaborated.

"I had to let Mandy Taft go last night. If business does pick up, I'm going to need more than just the two I have left."

"What happened with Mandy, if you don't mind my asking?" Lucy's radar was on high alert, given that Mandy was a solid suspect - in her opinion, even if Taylor didn't share her view.

Oliver sighed. "I've never seen a waitress mix up as many orders as that woman. She gets as many wrong in one night as she gets correct. We're hanging on by a thread over there, so I can't have bad customer service contributing to our problem."

"That's too bad," Lucy murmured. She stood up as Oliver rose from the table.

"It was nice to see you, Oliver. I'll send that price sheet over in a bit."

Oliver smiled, buttoning his coat back up. "Thank you, Lucy. I'm looking forward to doing business with you."

Lucy shook the hand he extended, watching out the window as Oliver made his way across the parking lot. She hoped Sizzle's business could be revived, but the damage might already have been done.

Unless Taylor was able to prove that Chef Fugasi was poisoned elsewhere.

22

After Oliver Crenshaw left, Lucy returned to the kitchen and the stack of orders waiting to be filled. Betsy was doing a fine job, taking her time and practicing her handwriting with the pastry bag before piping each message on individual cookie-grams.

Lucy, however, found herself terribly distracted. Her mind kept circling back around to everything that had happened in the last few days. She found herself replaying the visit she and Hannah had made to Wrigley's, and the waitress Marcia's revelations about Mandy and Chef Fugasi. Something niggled at the back of her mind, but she couldn't grasp on to it.

"So, Lucy, is that stray kitty still hanging around your house?" Betsy asked, and Lucy nodded.

"I visited Daphne's shelter to see if anyone had reported a missing grey and white tabby cat, but so far, no one has." She looked at Betsy with a gleam in her eye. "Any chance you'd be interested in adopting him?"

Betsy shook her head. "Not me, sorry. I can't have pets at my place. And Joseph has two cats already. Besides, you're not even sure yet if he's a stray, right?"

Lucy moved on to the next cookie, reading the order before she answered.

"No, it's hard to say, really. I can't even tell if it's a boy or a girl because he or she won't let me get close. I do think if it was a stray, it would be hungry enough to make human contact."

She piped the message onto the cookie-gram and reached for a box.

Betsy walked over to her table to switch her icing bag. "Have you tried asking Dr. Jax if he's heard of any missing cats?"

Lucy paused before answering. She wanted to say that Daphne probably would have told Dr. Jax, especially since the two were now dating, but she bit her tongue. It wasn't her secret to tell.

"Ah, no… not yet anyway. I haven't seen Dr. Jax since that night at Sizzle."

Betsy frowned, looking down at the cookie-gram Lucy was in the process of boxing. "Hey, boss, I hate to point this out, but that order is wrong. You used a chocolate cookie for a vanilla cookie order."

Lucy stared down at the order in question and saw Betsy was correct.

"Darn," she said, frowning. "You're right. Good catch, Betsy." She picked up a spatula, deciding to try and scrape the message off.

Betsy picked up the red icing bag and returned to her table. "Sorry, Lucy, I didn't catch the last thing you said about Dr. Jax."

"Oh." Lucy carefully slid the edge of the spatula under the royal icing, which was beginning to dry. "Um… Dr. Jax…" She stopped short, a sudden revelation coming to her, triggered by the mixed-up cookie-gram order.

"Oh, my goodness," she breathed, frozen in place, as several facts converged in her mind.

Dr. Jax had been dining at Sizzle the night of the murder. Daphne was secretly dating Dr. Jax. Bert Dobbins was one of the cooks at Sizzle, and Mandy was notorious for mixing up orders.

Could Bert Dobbins have found out about Daphne and Dr. Jax? Had he tried to poison the doctor, only to have Mandy mix up the order?

Could Bert really be a killer? Lucy thought of Bert's face when he'd seen Daphne at the bakery. His desperate, heartbroken expression…

In her heart of hearts, Lucy knew she was onto something. She slowly set down the spatula.

"Lucy?" Betsy sounded worried.

Lucy's mind was spinning. *Daphne said that Bert had accused her of being attracted to Dr. Jax before they'd even broken up. Had Bert spied on Daphne and seen her with the doctor?*

She realized Betsy was still staring at her. "I'm fine, Betsy. I just realized I need to talk to Taylor."

Lucy left the kitchen, heading for her office. She'd pulled her phone from her apron pocket and was dialing the station before she reached the staircase. Taylor's personal line went directly to voicemail.

Lucy tried his cell next. Same thing. "Darn it…" Lucy mumbled. *Where was he?*

She recalled their last conversation. Taylor had been investigating the vandalism at Dr. Jax's house. *Had Bert Dobbins been responsible for that?*

She needed to get to the station and talk to Taylor. If he wasn't there, she'd just wait for him.

She quickly walked back to the front room, grabbing her purse and keys from beneath the counter. "I've got an errand," she called to Aunt Tricia, who regarded her with a puzzled expression. "Be back soon."

Within minutes, she was on the road, heading for the Ivy Creek Police Station. As she pulled into their parking lot, she spotted Taylor's SUV. *Good, he was here.*

Lucy breezed through the door, making a beeline for Taylor's office. Just as her hand was poised to knock, he opened his office door, looking startled to see her.

"Hey. I just tried to call you back, and your Aunt Tricia said you stepped out on an errand."

Lucy nodded, brushing by him, and indicating he should shut the office door.

"I have a theory," she blurted out. "And please, let me tell you all of it before you say anything."

Lucy launched into the story of catching Dr. Jax and Daphne embracing at the animal shelter, and Taylor's eyes widened. She continued on, relaying Marcia's complaint about Mandy being a terrible waitress. At that point Taylor frowned, looking lost.

He opened his mouth to speak, but Lucy held up a hand to let her finish. Taylor settled back in his chair, folding his arms and listening as she shared the details about Oliver Crenshaw's visit to the bakery, ending with Mandy being fired for mixing up orders.

"So, don't you see?" she asked excitedly. "Bert Dobbins was cooking that night at Sizzle. And Dr. Jax was on a regular schedule to come in for his free dinners. Bert could have found out about Daphne and Dr. Jax—it all makes sense if you think about it. The prowler, and Dr. Jax's property being vandalized—that all happened after Daphne and Dr. Jax started dating. So what if Bert decided to poison the doctor?"

Taylor interrupted, looking doubtful. "And Mandy served the poisoned steak to Chef Fugasi by mistake? That's quite a stretch, Lucy. There's no evidence to support your theory."

He shook his head. "We have both motive and opportunity with Mrs. Fugasi—double motive, really, with the chef's infidelity as well as the life insurance policy. I'm planning on calling Mrs. Fugasi into the station for a formal interview."

Lucy stared at him. "Aren't you at least going to talk to Bert? See if he acts suspicious?"

Taylor stood up. Lucy could tell he was struggling to hide his irritation. "At some point, I may do that, but right now, I have my hands full running down this lead." He looked at Lucy's face and softened his tone.

"Honey, you're getting way too deep into this. Why don't you just leave it all alone, and focus on the bakery? I'm making progress on the case. This murder will not go unsolved, I assure you."

Lucy felt deflated. "I'm just trying to help you," she protested. "I'll bet if you just talked to Bert-"

There was a knock on Taylor's office door at that moment, and he held up a finger to Lucy, crossing the room to open it. The officer standing in the doorway spoke in a low tone and Taylor nodded his head. He turned back to Lucy as the man left.

She stood up. "I know, I know, you have work to do." She sighed. "Please consider having a chat with Bert Dobbins. I don't think I'm wrong about this. I have a feeling."

She kissed him on the cheek and exited his office, walking through the lobby to the front door. As she stepped outside, she took a deep breath, frustrated to her very core.

If Bert *was* the killer, motivated by deadly jealousy, he wasn't going to just let it go. If he was behind the vandalism at the doctor's house, it only proved his rage was still burning hot. Dr. Jax might be in real danger.

But what could she do?

23

*L*ucy stood at her bedroom window, staring out at the night. She couldn't relax.

She'd tried a hot bubble bath, reading in her favorite chair, and listening to soft music, but she felt fidgety and on edge. The possibility that Bert Dobbins could have nefarious intent toward one of her favorite people in Ivy Creek was chilling. Lucy hugged her arms to her sides and shivered.

Was Bert out there right now, on his way to Dr. Jax's place? Would he break into the house this time?

Feeling powerless was not something that sat well with her. She felt like her hands were tied. Taylor wasn't ready to investigate Bert as a suspect. And she, herself, couldn't exactly warn Dr. Jax—it would be slander to implicate Bert publicly, without any proof.

Lucy sat down on the bed and then jumped up again. She couldn't just sit here worrying. She had to do something, anything. Maybe if she drove by Dr. Jax's house, she could reassure herself that everything was fine.

Deciding that option was her best course of action, Lucy traded her pajamas for street clothes again, and left her bedroom, tiptoeing down the hallway. Aunt Tricia was already in bed. With any luck, she would be back before her aunt even noticed.

Lucy shrugged into her parka and grabbed her phone and keys, letting herself out the kitchen door. The night was clear and cold, jewel-like stars twinkling in a black velvet sky. She could see her breath puff out as mist as she started the car and backed down the driveway.

It was after eleven and the sleepy town of Ivy Creek had all but rolled up the carpet. Solitary lights flickered here and there in people's houses, but the downtown area was deserted, the shopfronts appearing cold and dark.

Lucy made her way over to the Hemingford Estates neighborhood, peering at the house numbers on mailboxes illuminated by her headlights. For a long time, Dr. Jax had operated his veterinary practice at his home address, and Lucy had been there several times before. She slowed down as she got close, scoping out the surrounding area to see if she saw any suspicious vehicles.

1224. There was Dr. Jax's house. His Ford Ranger was in the driveway, and there was a light burning in the living room. Lucy winced inwardly, seeing his garage with its bashed-in windows taped up with cardboard.

She slowed to a crawl, taking a good look around, but didn't see anything out of place. Sighing with relief, she headed out of the neighborhood, intending to take a left to go back home.

A little voice sounded inside her head. *What if Bert was waiting until it was a little later? It wasn't even midnight yet. He'd probably wait until he thought the doctor was asleep.*

Lucy tried to banish the thought. Obviously, she couldn't stake out Dr. Jax's house indefinitely. She had no idea if or when Bert was planning to return—or if it had even been Bert doing the vandalizing, for that matter.

She drummed her fingers on the steering wheel, thinking. Come to think of it, she didn't even know if Bert was working, or off tonight. If he was working, Dr. Jax was probably safe. And maybe tomorrow she could have another talk with Taylor and convince him to at least question Bert.

Lucy knew Bert lived close to her own side of town, on Devonshire Avenue. She decided she'd drive by his house on her way back home to see if he was there. If Bert's car was gone, he was probably at work.

In ten minutes, Lucy had turned onto Bert's street. She drove slowly down its length, looking out for his red Jeep Wrangler. She almost missed it, driving past it before catching a glimpse of the red vehicle in her rear-view mirror.

She turned around at the end of the street, backtracking, and soon drew abreast of Bert's residence. She pulled off to the side and turned off her headlights, studying the house.

Lights were blazing in every room, and she could see a man's silhouette, pacing back and forth behind the living room curtain. Lucy squinted at the scene, frowning. At one point, the figure—who she presumed was Bert—started waving his arms as if he were arguing with someone not visible from her vantage point.

Lucy's gaze bounced to Bert's driveway, empty except for his own vehicle. *Who was in there with him?* Unease prickled down her spine. Something wasn't right.

The silhouette moved out of sight. Lucy watched as the lights extinguished in the house, one by one. The residence was now completely dark.

Suddenly, the porch light snapped on, and Lucy watched as Bert exited the house. He held a black duffel bag in one hand as he locked the door, casting furtive glances at the neighboring houses.

Lucy shrank down in her seat, praying Bert wouldn't notice her across the street. Her heart pounded. *What would she say if he came over to her car?*

She heard his vehicle start and the wash of headlights passed over her. Lucy held her breath, frozen in place, until she heard his Jeep drive away. She popped back up, seeing his taillights at the end of the street, and hurried to start her car.

She drove to the end of the street and looked left and right, catching a glimpse of the red Jeep driving in the same direction she'd just come from.

Lucy's heart sank. *That was the way to Dr. Jax's house!*

She turned left, following Bert and biting her lip. *Was he on his way to Dr. Jax's house? Should she call Taylor?* Lucy felt around on the passenger seat, locating her phone. She paused, with her thumb on the power button.

She'd be jumping the gun if she called for help now. She didn't know where Bert was going. He might just be out for a drive, or off to visit a friend—though that was unlikely, given the hour. But if the police got involved and it turned out to be a false alarm, Lucy would be viewed as crying wolf. No one would believe her theory, and worse, her pointing a finger too early might even help Bert evade suspicion.

She decided she'd wait to call in the cavalry. She had her phone and if Bert drove to Dr. Jax's house, she'd call the police immediately.

Lucy concentrated on following Bert, trying to keep at a safe distance. Within five minutes, they'd passed the turn for Dr. Jax's house, and Lucy breathed a sigh of relief. *But where was Bert going?* He seemed to be heading out of town.

Before too long, the red Jeep turned down a gravel road at the edge of town. Lucy knew this road. It only led to one place - Dilworth Memorial Bridge. Lucy hesitated, stopping on the primary road, considering her options.

Should she follow him?

24

There were only two reasons Lucy could think of that Bert would drive down that road at this time of night. One: to hide evidence by tossing it in the river. And two… the second option was tragic, but Lucy knew it was a possibility.

The area surrounding Dilworth Memorial Bridge had been made infamous decades before, earning the nickname "Suicide Point". As depressed as Bert had been since Daphne had broken his heart, it wasn't unlikely, to Lucy's way of thinking, that he may be there to end his own life.

Lucy turned down the road, picking up her cell phone. *Better to play it safe.* She could always say she'd been mistaken.

Dialing 911, she held the phone with one hand while navigating the bumpy road with the other.

"911. What's your emergency?"

Lucy cleared her throat. "I just saw a man climb up on Dilworth Bridge. I think he might be suicidal."

A JUICY STEAK TRAGEDY

"Can I have your name, please?"

Lucy hesitated, then clicked the disconnect button, laying the phone down on the seat. She'd made the call, which was the important thing.

Up ahead, she could see Bert's vehicle, parked off to one side. She slowed, flicking off her headlights and crawling forward. She didn't see Bert anywhere. *Was he on foot, on his way up the bridge?*

She stopped the car, straining her eyes to see in the darkness. Nothing seemed to be moving. Deciding she'd be better able to investigate on foot herself, she parked her car and eased out, shutting the door softly.

The night was chilly, and she zipped her jacket, retrieving her gloves from the pockets and donning them. The breeze coming off the river whipped her hair into a mess, and she shivered, wishing she'd worn a hat.

Lucy crept forward, keeping to the edge of the gravel road nearest the bushes, trying to remain unseen. She reached Bert's Jeep and sidled up to it, peering inside. Besides the black duffel bag lying on the front seat, the vehicle was empty. He was on foot, then.

She stepped to the edge of the river, peering up at the massive bridge. It was illuminated in twenty-foot sections, and she squinted at the structure, trying to determine if there was anyone climbing up the trestle.

Suddenly, she heard a noise in the bushes behind her. She whirled around, her heart in her throat.

Bert Dobbins stood there, his eyes glassy and wild, his coat unzipped despite the February chill.

"Daphne!" he cried out, launching himself at her.

Lucy staggered backward in shock, but it was too late. The man's arms wrapped around her in a bear hug, and she could smell the sour sweat on his clothes. His face pressed into her neck, and the wetness of his tears fell on her skin. Lucy struggled to get free.

"I'm not Daphne!" She pushed at him, panicking. "It's me, Lucy Hale!"

Bert seemed not to hear her. Lucy's fists pummeled him, but he seemed not to care, smoothly turning her in his strong grasp until he held her arms pinned to her sides, embracing her from behind. He squeezed her tightly to still her movements, and Lucy fought to breathe.

"Oh Daphne, I'm so sorry," he sobbed onto her shoulder. "I've done a terrible thing."

"Help!" Lucy screamed, finally managing to draw in a deep breath. She was terrified, realizing Bert had completely lost touch with reality. "Help me! Somebody help me!"

"I never meant to hurt Chef Fugasi," Bert confessed, his broken tone conveying his misery. "Please don't hate me, Daphne. I just wanted to be with you. But now there's an innocent man's blood on my hands. How can I live with that?" His plaintive wail echoed through the night.

"How can I go on, Daphne? All the dreams I had for our future, all the plans I'd made, just vanished in an instant. And why? I just don't understand why. Everything was going fine. We were happy…. Weren't we happy, Daphne?"

Lucy tried jabbing Bert in the ribs with her elbow, kicking and yelling, but he just tightened his arms around her sides. It became more difficult to breathe, and her struggles slowed.

"Please, Bert," Lucy wheezed out. "Bert... Listen to me... you're confused."

"I never dreamed I'd be able to win a woman like you," Bert babbled on morosely. "When you first told me you loved me, I couldn't believe my luck! And I vowed to always make you feel loved and safe in our relationship. I totally cherished you, Daphne. Where did I go wrong? Why did you stop loving me?"

Lucy began to feel lightheaded, panting out shallow breaths, unable to do anything to loosen Bert's grasp. *I can't pass out*, she told herself. *I need to get enough oxygen to stay conscious. Focus on breathing.*

"It was all Dr. Jax's fault," Bert's voice turned angry. "He deserved to die. We were so happy until he came along. I knew the minute you met him that your heart was already turning cold toward me. And then he swooped in and took you away from me." Bert started to weep again. "I need you, Daphne. I don't want to go on without you."

Lucy felt his arms loosen a little bit in his grief, and she drew a deep breath. "Bert," she tried again, speaking urgently. "Please, let me help you."

She tried to turn to face him, and he tightened his arms reflexively. Once more, it felt like steel bands were wrapped around her ribcage.

"That stupid waitress," he growled. "Of all the orders to mix up! And now what do I do, Daphne? I've seen you with him, you know. At his house, at the shelter. I've watched the two of you... laughing at me..." His words ended on a sob.

Lucy tried frantically to think of something to say to bring Bert out of his delusion. She knew it was only a matter of time before authorities showed up in response to her 911 call. She just had to wait it out. She needed to buy some time before he did something unthinkable.

"Bert," she croaked hoarsely, but suddenly, he started walking, pushing her in front of him.

Horrified, Lucy realized he was forcing her into the river. "No!" she tried to scream, struggling anew, but her scream was a pitiful wheeze, carried away by the wind.

"Shh…" Bert whispered in her ear. Her struggles were completely ineffectual as he proceeded forward, splashing into the frigid river. "It's for the best, Daphne. This way, we'll be together forever."

25

The icy water seeped into Lucy's clothes, stealing her breath away with the shock of it. She kicked her feet and screamed, unable to loosen his grip as they waded deeper. Her feet became numb almost instantly.

"Stop! No, Bert! Let me go!" Lucy despaired, feeling the icy water creep up to her waist. She was frantic now, aware that hypothermia was as real of a risk as drowning. *She had to get free!*

"I'm sorry it has to be this way, Daphne," Bert's voice sounded slurred, and Lucy knew the cold was affecting him as well. Pain stabbed like tiny daggers into her legs as the icy water stole her warmth.

Her body felt leaden, and she tried to move her legs in vain. Her feet were completely numb. If Bert were to suddenly release her, she wasn't sure she'd be able to stand. The thought of going under terrified her.

Was she destined to drown here, in the shadow of Dilworth Memorial Bridge, with a raving lunatic calling her another woman's name?

"B-Bert," Lucy managed to stutter. Her teeth were chattering violently. "We have to g-get out of the water."

He didn't respond, and Lucy tried to wiggle free. As numb as she was, she couldn't be sure if he was still grasping her as tightly. She'd lost almost all feeling in her lower body.

"B-Bert!" Lucy cried hoarsely. There was no response. Unable to swivel around, but needing to get his attention, Lucy leaned back heavily against him, unprepared when his body simply gave way.

Icy water doused her head, the shock of it feeling like a slap to the face. Lucy bobbed back up, trying to feel her feet underneath her. She flailed her arms, desperate to not submerge completely, and found Bert was no longer holding her.

In her peripheral vision, she could see the shadowy form of Bert's body, floating in the murky water. The current spun him away, toward the middle of the river. *Was he dead or simply unconscious?*

Lucy tried to make her way back to the shore, her uncooperative limbs limiting her ability to move. She fixed her gaze on dry ground, only fifteen feet away, though it seemed like a mile. Slowly, she managed to point herself in that direction, but found herself moving with agonizing slowness. She drifted a little, and her mind began to grow fuzzy.

When she first heard the sirens, she thought it was merely her ears ringing. The flashing lights brought her out of her fog as emergency vehicles barreled down the gravel road.

In a stupor brought on by hypothermia, Lucy gazed uncomprehendingly at the bi-colored lights reflecting on the water's surface. Blue, then red, then blue.

Someone called her name, and she raised her head, stunned to find herself lying in the shallow water, clutching at the reeds, her face inches away from the muddy bank. Her legs were splayed out behind her, still half-submerged.

"Lucy!" A familiar voice shouted her name again, and she tried to answer, but was unable to relax her clenched jaw. Splashes sounded nearby and she saw Taylor rushing toward her.

"We need the thermal blanket here, and a stretcher!" he yelled, before reaching down and scooping Lucy up into his arms. He cradled her to his chest and carried her ashore.

Lucy clung to him, greedy for his body's warmth. "Taylor?"

She hoped this wasn't her imagination. Everything had a surreal feeling to it, and the thought occurred to her that she might be dreaming.

"I'm right here, honey. You're going to be OK."

Lucy felt the blanket being wrapped around her, and she was lowered to the stretcher. Someone pulled a wool cap over her head. Her teeth began chattering violently again as her body started to thaw.

"Bert," she managed to say. Taylor took her frozen hands in his, rubbing them briskly.

"Where is Bert?" Taylor asked, his tone terse. "Do you know?"

Lucy suddenly felt overwhelmingly sleepy. "River..." she mumbled.

Taylor spoke briskly. "Stay with me, Lucy. Don't go to sleep. How are you feeling? Can you feel this?"

Lucy shook her head. She just wanted to sleep. She imagined she was in her own bed, warm and toasty beneath her down comforter.

"Open your eyes, Lucy. The EMT wants to check your pupils."

Dutifully, Lucy opened her eyes, frowning as the flashlight beam shone in her face. She heard Taylor turn to his officers, directing them to search the riverbank for Bert.

Someone tucked another blanket around her and pressed something warm into her hands. The fragrant scent of coffee woke her up a little, and she gratefully took a sip. As coffee went, it was burned and stale, but Lucy thought it might be one of the best things she'd ever tasted.

Pins and needles started stabbing in her extremities as her flesh warmed, and she shifted uncomfortably.

Taylor finished directing his men, and turned back to Lucy, cradling her head in his warm hands. "Feeling better?"

She nodded. "I just want to soak in a hot bath for an hour or two." She looked hopefully up at his face. "Will you take me home?"

Taylor shook his head ruefully. "I'm afraid you need to go to the hospital and get checked out, honey. I'll call your aunt to bring you a change of clothes."

A JUICY STEAK TRAGEDY

Lucy sighed, knowing he was right. She still couldn't feel her feet, though the pinprick sensations were now traveling down her calves. The EMTs hoisted the stretcher, preparing to load her into the ambulance.

Lucy turned her head to gaze at the icy river, its blackness appearing malevolent and hungry.

Where was Bert Dobbins?

26

"Achoo!" Lucy sneezed into her handkerchief, spooking Gigi, who'd been nestled on her lap. Gigi ran down the hall as though the devil were after her, and Taylor chuckled.

"What a brave and fearless creature," he joked, and Betsy giggled.

Betsy and Joseph sat on the loveseat in Lucy's living room, with Hannah and Miles perched on the sofa. Lucy had been kept overnight at the hospital, monitored for frostbite and hypothermia. She'd been released the next morning and slept an entire day. Today was the first day she'd been able to have visitors, and she'd woken up with a terrible head cold.

Aunt Tricia walked briskly into the room, setting down a mug of hot tea laced with honey in front of Lucy. "Are you sure you should be out of bed?"

Lucy nodded her head. "I'm fine, Auntie. I sound worse than I feel."

Aunt Tricia eyed Lucy critically before taking a seat in the easy chair. "If you say so."

Hannah cleared her throat. "Speaking of brave and fearless… explain to me, Lucy, why you didn't call me to stake out Bert's house with you? You know I'm always up for an adventure." Miles regarded her with an eyebrow raised and she winked at him, patting his knee reassuringly.

"I guess I should have," Lucy admitted. "At the time, I just wanted to make sure Dr. Jax was OK. I really wasn't planning to go near Bert Dobbins' house." She picked up her mug and gratefully sipped the steaming beverage.

Taylor frowned. "You could have been killed, Lucy." He turned to address the others. "We found a duffel bag in Bert's truck containing zip ties, duct tape, and a stun gun. I think Bert may have been planning to kidnap Dr. Jax."

"Or Daphne," Lucy added. "I guess we'll never know what he was intending to do, or to whom. I still believe he'd gone to the river to commit suicide."

Taylor nodded. "From what you told me, he was suffering so much guilt from Chef Fugasi's death, maybe he decided he couldn't go through with another murder."

Betsy shivered. "Has the body the police found downstream been positively identified?"

Taylor nodded. "It was Bert. Dental records confirmed it. Cause of death was technically a heart attack, though the coroner says it was brought on by his exposure to the freezing temperatures."

The group was silent for a moment, counting their blessings. It could have been Lucy, washed up on a riverbank.

"Tell them what else you guys found when you searched Bert's house," Lucy urged Taylor. Gigi trotted back into the room and leapt up on Lucy's lap, kneading the fuzzy blanket and purring.

The group turned inquisitive eyes to Taylor. "We found the same pesticide that poisoned Chef Fugasi, stored in Bert's cellar," he informed them. "As well as a plastic squeeze bottle containing traces of Sizzle's marinade—in which the pesticide was also present."

"So, it looks like I was right," Lucy pointed out, unable to help herself. "Bert was intending to poison Dr. Jax, but Mandy mixed up the orders."

Hannah stared at her. "Oh, my goodness, Lucy. The four of us were dining there that night! If Chef Fugasi's death was that random... it could have been any one of us."

The grim revelation hung in the air, sobering them. Miles turned to Hannah, seeking to lighten the mood. "That would have made for a heck of a first date."

Hannah cast him a look, rolling her eyes, though the corners of her mouth tugged upward.

Lucy pulled her blanket a little more snugly around herself before commenting to Taylor. "Mrs. Fugasi's life insurance settlement must be above suspicion, now. I have to say, I'm glad. I think that poor woman has been through enough."

"I can't imagine being in a marriage like that," Betsy said. "I don't understand that mindset, choosing to pretend you don't notice your spouse's infidelities."

"That's not my idea of marriage, either," Joseph remarked quietly, and Betsy flashed him a smile, squeezing his hand.

"So, how's the play going with the new Romeo?" Hannah asked Joseph. "I know it sounds morbid, but the scandal of your former lead actor being a murderer will probably boost your ticket sales."

Joseph nodded. "Yeah, you're probably right. People are funny like that. Justin King is doing a great job, though." He looked around the room. "When are you all coming to the theater? The play only runs another two weekends."

Betsy pointed out. "Lucy needs to get over her cold first." She caught Taylor's eye. "Of course you'll be taking her, won't you, Taylor? That would make for a romantic Valentine's Night out."

Taylor fidgeted. "Well, I'm not sure. It's kind of a girly production, isn't it? Probably Tricia and Lucy will go together." He looked hopefully at Lucy.

Lucy wasn't letting him off the hook. "I would love for you to take me to see Romeo and Juliet, Taylor." She sneezed again, and Gigi jumped down, stalking off towards the kitchen.

Taylor relented, with a tender look directed at Lucy. "Whatever makes you happy," he said, taking her hand and kissing it. "Your wish is my command."

Lucy smiled at him, gazing into his blue eyes. The foolish worries she'd had in the last couple of weeks - brought on by the silly magazine quiz - vanished, replaced by a warm glow of love. Taylor was always there for her when she needed him. That's what mattered.

"It's a date," she said. "As soon as I'm better."

The next morning, Lucy was the first one awake. Wrapping her robe around herself, she padded out to the kitchen, feeling a bit better than she had the day before. Yawning, she opened the cabinet and looked around for Gigi. The cat was usually tapping Lucy's leg by now, demanding her morning treat. Lucy glanced at the kitchen door and saw Gigi sitting in front of the window, tail swishing.

Uh-oh.

Lucy walked over to peer out as well. The gray kitty sat inches away from the low window panels, staring back at Gigi intently. His ears were up, not back, and he crouched in a non-intimidating manner. Lucy was surprised and relieved to see the feline now sported a brand new, red leather collar.

"So, you do have a home," she murmured, pleased. Gigi touched her nose to the glass, trying to sniff the other cat, and the gray kitty did the same.

Astonished, Lucy watched Gigi turn from the window and poke her head through the kitty door, taking the strange cat's measure before cautiously crawling through.

The gray kitty remained still and watchful as Gigi lowered herself to the cobblestone patio, tucking her legs beneath herself, mirroring his pose. The two regarded each other curiously, with only a foot between them.

Smiling, Lucy turned away to prepare the coffee before Aunt Tricia woke up. *It looked like Gigi had a new friend.*

As she scooped coffee grounds into the filter, Lucy's phone buzzed in her robe pocket. She fished it out, glancing at the screen. It was a text message from Betsy, with an attachment.

She clicked on it, and read Betsy's message, causing a smile to bloom on her face from ear to ear.

He loves me!

Lucy opened the attachment. It was a picture of a Sweet Delights cookie-gram, decorated in Hannah's professional style, apparently sent to Betsy from Joseph. Lucy recognized the quote from a poem by Christopher Marlowe, outlined in a heart shape.

"Come live with me and be my love"

Lucy sent a heart emoji as a response, then tucked the phone back in her pocket, her soul filled with happiness for her friend. She hummed as she set the coffee to brew.

Love is grand.

The End

SWEET DELIGHTS BAKERY'S COOKIE-GRAMS

Ingredients

1 cup unsalted butter, softened
1 cup granulated sugar
2 tsp. vanilla extract
2 large eggs at room temperature
2 1/2 cups all-purpose flour
3/4 tsp. baking powder
1/2 tsp. salt

Procedure

Beat butter with sugar until smooth, add vanilla extract. Mix well. Beat in eggs, one at a time. Continue beating until mixture is fluffy, scraping the sides with a rubber spatula.

In a small bowl, combine flour, baking powder, and salt, stirring with a wire whisk (or sift the ingredients together)

Add dry ingredients to the first mixture, stirring until well combined. Be sure to scrape the sides of the bowl – unblended sugar/butter mixture will ruin your cookies.

Turn dough on to a piece of plastic wrap or waxed paper, wrap and flatten slightly (to speed the chilling process). Chill dough until somewhat firm and easy to handle.

Roll dough out on floured surface to 1/4 inch thick. Cut rectangles of the appropriate size for your own cookie-grams. Suggested size is 4" x 6".

Using a spatula, transfer cookies to a parchment-lined baking sheet. Straighten cookie edges as necessary.

Bake in a 375-degree F oven for 8–10 minutes, until edges begin to brown slightly. Remove from oven and cool completely. Decorate with royal icing.

ROYAL ICING

Ingredients

4 cups sifted confectioners' sugar
6 TBL warm water
3 TBL meringue powder (can be found in Walmart or some grocery stores' baking aisle)

Procedure

Whisk together meringue powder in water in mixing bowl, using a fork or small whisk. Add confectioners' sugar slowly, mixing by hand till all is somewhat incorporated.

Beat on medium-high speed with electric mixture until stiff peaks form (approx. 7 minutes)

Tint to desired colors using gel dyes for best consistency. If using liquid dye, you may need to thicken icing with additional sugar.

Pipe onto cookie-grams and let dry for one hour.

AFTERWORD

Thank you for reading **A Juicy Steak Tragedy**. I really hope you enjoyed reading it as much as I had writing it!

If you have a minute, please consider leaving a review on Amazon or the retailer where you got it.

Many thanks in advance for your support!

SOUTHERN FRIED AND GRIEF STRICKEN

CHAPTER 1 SNEAK PEEK

CHAPTER 1 SNEAK PEEK

"Can you believe it's already been fifteen years since we graduated?" Lucy looked over her shoulder at Hannah, who was straightening the bakery displays. "Where did the time go?"

Hannah shook her head. "It's crazy. It seems like yesterday that we were taking classes with Professor Sprague. He was my favorite teacher."

Lucy smiled at the memory. "Mine, too. It will be so great to see him again." She glanced at the clock and then opened the cash register to stock the till. Only ten minutes before they opened.

Sweet Delights Bakery was Lucy's pride and joy. She'd taken over the business nearly two years ago, after the unexpected passing of both of her parents. She'd floundered a bit at first, but thankfully, Hannah had stopped in at the perfect moment, looking for work. Lucy now relied on the other woman, every single day, for both her skill in the kitchen and her practical nature.

"What a great honor," Hannah remarked, tying on her apron. "To have the entire new wing of the building dedicated to him. He must be tickled pink." She poured a cup of coffee, adding a shot of hazelnut syrup.

"Is Miles coming to the dedication ceremony?" Lucy asked. She knew Hannah's boyfriend had his hands full these days, helping out at the Ivy Creek Theater, as well as the local animal shelter.

Hannah smiled, nodding. "Yes. He called me last night. He'll be accompanying me to both the reunion and the dedication ceremony the next day. He got one of the college students from the theater to fill his slot at the shelter."

Lucy grinned. "And how are things going with you two?" She was thrilled that Hannah had finally found someone to make her happy. The two had begun dating right around Valentine's Day and were practically inseparable.

"Better and better every day," Hannah turned to face Lucy, her face uncharacteristically serious. "Sometimes I can't believe how compatible we are. I never thought I'd find a man who loved animals as much as I do… but here he is!"

"Aww… another happily-ever-after story," Lucy teased. "Following in Betsy's footsteps."

Betsy was Lucy's youngest employee, several years behind Lucy and Hannah. She'd fallen head-over-heels for the town's theater director, Joseph Hiller, and they'd recently decided to move in together.

"Speaking of Betsy, how are we going to cover the front counter while she's gone? They'll be gone two weeks to visit Betsy's family, right?" Hannah looked worried.

The bakery was a popular stop for a lot of Ivy Creek citizens, and there were days they could barely keep up, even when fully staffed by Lucy, Hannah, Betsy, and Lucy's Aunt Tricia.

Lucy sighed. "We'll get by. Sorry, Hannah, I know it will mean extra work for all of us, but I didn't have the heart to tell Betsy no. Honestly, my main concern is that Aunt Tricia will overdo it. After all, she's no spring chicken—but don't tell her I said that!"

Hannah looked past Lucy towards the parking lot. "Speak of the devil. Here she is now."

Lucy turned to see Aunt Tricia coming up the sidewalk. Although her aunt was still active, attending her book club meetings and working five days a week manning the bakery counter, Lucy could see tell-tale signs that the woman was slowing down. Arthritis had begun to creep into her limbs, and even though Aunt Tricia never complained, Lucy had observed her moving stiffly in the morning, especially during the cold Colorado winter months.

Lucy hurried to finish their conversation. "I think while Betsy's gone, one of us should help her at the counter during the morning rush and the lunch rush. Hopefully, we won't get too many custom orders this week, and the baking will be light."

Hannah nodded, holding up crossed fingers, just as the bell tinkled and Aunt Tricia walked in.

"Well, good morning, my lovelies," Aunt Tricia greeted them, unbuttoning her coat. Mid-April in Colorado, though sunny and bright, was still chilly enough to warrant bundling up.

Lucy raised her eyebrows at the sweet salutation. Aunt Tricia seemed to be in a very good mood, indeed. "Good morning, Auntie." She was echoed by Hannah.

Aunt Tricia hung up her coat and tied on an apron. "So, what do we have for specials today?" She smiled brightly at Lucy.

Lucy listed what she thought they should offer, all the while studying Aunt Tricia's expression. Something was up.

She didn't have long to wait. Before she was even through with the breakfast specials, Aunt Tricia interrupted her.

"Wonderful, wonderful. That all sounds perfect. By the way…" Aunt Tricia turned and fiddled with the cappuccino machine.

Lucy waited a few beats, but her aunt did not continue. "Yes, Auntie?"

Aunt Tricia turned, her countenance determinedly cheerful. "I made a huge sale this morning!"

Lucy was stymied. "This morning?" It was still so early.

Aunt Tricia nodded. "As I was getting into my car, our neighbor Cassie was picking up her newspaper. You'll never guess what she said!" She looked at Lucy expectantly.

Lucy asked cautiously, "Ah… I don't know. What did she say?"

Aunt Tricia stacked and divided the café napkins next to the syrups, then re-stacked them. She seemed a bit nervous.

"Well, apparently Margot Trotter was supposed to plan the menu for the reunion and dedication ceremony, but she forgot one thing. One very important thing. The desserts."

Lucy had a sinking feeling for what her aunt was going to say next. She exchanged a look with Hannah, whose brow was creased with worry.

"Oh?" Lucy replied, bracing herself.

Aunt Tricia nodded vigorously. "All of those out-of-towners and alumni, coming in for the events, and not finding the teeniest bit of sweets offered… well, I couldn't let that happen!"

Lucy sighed. "OK, Aunt Tricia. How many desserts are we providing?" How bad could it be?

Aunt Tricia looked at Lucy over the rim of her glasses. "Fifty pecan pies…"

Lucy sighed. Not great news, with them being short-staffed, but it could be worse.

"OK." She nodded, her mind running through the supplies needed. "We can do that."

Aunt Tricia bit her lip, adding. "Fifty for the reunion. And twenty more for the dedication."

Lucy's eyes widened. She heard Hannah snort with laughter before walking away.

Aunt Tricia looked at Lucy's shocked face, and hurried to say, "What great exposure for the bakery, Lucy! It will pay off in the long run, you'll see."

"I sure hope so," Lucy mumbled. "Why so many pecan pies? Pecans are expensive, you know." She was horrified by a sudden thought. "Auntie, tell me you did not say we'd do this for free."

Aunt Tricia frowned. "Of course not! But I gave them a bulk discount. Twenty percent off."

Lucy groaned, turning away. The next two weeks were going to be hectic enough, already, and now this. But there was nothing to be done about it now.

The telephone rang, and Lucy welcomed the chance to step away before she said something to Aunt Tricia she'd regret.

"Good morning, Sweet Delights Bakery. How may I help you?"

A vaguely familiar voice addressed her by name.

"Lucy?"

She frowned. "Yes, this is she." Who could it be?

The man cleared his throat, continuing, "Splendid! Lucy, this is Mayor Yeats. I need to ask you a personal favor regarding the upcoming reunion."

Lucy's grip tightened on the receiver.

Now what?

SOUTHERN FRIED AND GRIEF STRICKEN

AN IVY CREEK COZY MYSTERY

RUTH BAKER

ALSO BY RUTH BAKER

The Ivy Creek Cozy Mystery Series

Which Pie Goes with Murder? (Book 1)

Twinkle, Twinkle, Deadly Sprinkles (Book 2)

Waffles and Scuffles (Book 3)

Silent Night, Unholy Bites (Book 4)

Waffles and Scuffles (Book 5)

Cookie Dough and Bruised Egos (Book 6)

A Sticky Toffee Catastrophe (Book 7)

Dough Shall Not Murder (Book 8)

Deadly Bites on Winter Nights (Book 9)

A Juicy Steak Tragedy (Book 10)

Southern Fried and Grief Stricken (Book 11)

NEWSLETTER SIGNUP

Want **FREE** COPIES OF FUTURE **CLEANTALES** BOOKS, FIRST NOTIFICATION OF NEW RELEASES, CONTESTS AND GIVEAWAYS?

GO TO THE LINK BELOW TO SIGN UP TO THE NEWSLETTER!

https://cleantales.com/newsletter/

Printed in Dunstable, United Kingdom